Cosmic Commandos

Cosmic
Comm

CHRISTOPHER ELIOPOULOS

DIAL BOOKS FOR YOUNG READERS

DIAL BOOKS FOR YOUNG READERS
PENGUIN YOUNG READERS GROUP • An imprint of Penguin Random House LLC
375 Hudson Street • New York, NY 10014

Printed in China
ISBN 9781101994481 • 10 9 8 7 6 5 4 3 2 1

Design by Jason Henry
The artwork for this book was created digitally.

For Jeremy and Justin,
my heroes

CHAPTER ONE

A STINKISH LIFE

THESE ARE MY STINKISH PARENTS.
MY MOM IS SUPER MEAN.
AND I THINK MY DAD NEVER HAD FUN IN HIS ENTIRE LIFE.
THEY DON'T LET ME DO OR HAVE ANYTHING.

OKAY, OKAY. THIS IS WHAT THEY *REALLY* LOOK LIKE, BUT I STILL WONDER ABOUT MY *GENE POOL*.
I ADMIT, THEY REALLY AREN'T EVIL, BUT BOY ARE THEY *BORING*.
HOW CAN YOU WATCH COOKING SHOWS ON TV *EVERY NIGHT*?
#2 DAD WE TRY HARDER!

JEREMY, TURN THAT OFF!
IT'S TIME FOR BREAKFAST!
THIS IS MY WHOLE LIFE.
EVERYONE TELLS ME WHAT TO DO AND I *NEVER* GET TO DO WHAT *I* WANT.
GET UP.
BRUSH YOUR TEETH.
EAT YOUR BREAKFAST!
GO TO SCHOOL.

EAT YOUR LUNCH.
EEEWWW, IS THIS VOMIT MAC & CHEESE?
HAND IN YOUR TESTS.
DO YOUR HOMEWORK.
EAT YOUR DINNER.
YUCK! WAS THIS COOKED IN THE GARBAGE?
GO TO BED.
SEE? ALWAYS TELLING ME WHAT TO DO.
NOW WATCH WHAT HAPPENS WHEN I ASK FOR SOMETHING. A SMALL, SAFE, AND COOL SOMETHING.

MOM, CAN I HAVE A HIGH-POWERED, LASER-BLASTING, PELLET-SHOOTING, COSMIC COMMANDO RIFLE?
NO.
BUT, MOOOOOM, WHY NOT? ALL MY FRIENDS HAVE ONE!
IT SHOOTS FOUR DIFFERENT KINDS OF DARTS, HAS A TOW-LINE, A GRAPPLING HOOK, AND A WATER-SQUIRTER!
I DON'T **CARE** ABOUT YOUR FRIENDS.
I DON'T WANT GUNS IN THIS HOUSE. YOU COULD HURT SOMEONE.

BUT...
BUT, MOM...
...IT'S A FAKE GUN!
IT CAN'T HURT ANYONE!
I SAID NO.
FINE!
THEN, CAN I HAVE A COSMIC COMMANDO GRENADE LAUNCHER?
JEREMY, I HAVE WORK TO DO AND-

MOM, IF I DON'T GET IT I'M GONNA DIE!
OH, I HIGHLY DOUBT THAT.
KAKK!
GASP!
THUD!

VERY CONVINCING. NOW GO GET READY FOR SCHOOL...AND GET YOUR **BROTHER**.
SEE?
NOTHING. I GET **NOTHING**.
I DON'T GET VIDEO GAMES...
...OR COOL WEAPONS!
THE ONLY THINGS I SEEM TO GET ARE THE THINGS I ***DON'T*** WANT.
LIKE, SAY, MY BROTHER.
MY ***TWIN*** BROTHER.
IDENTICAL TWIN.
IDENTICAL, EXCEPT ***I'M*** NORMAL.

THIS IS JUSTIN. HE'S ALWAYS DOING SOMETHING TO EMBARRASS ME.
SKRITCH SKRATCH
ARGH!! SEE?! SEE?!!

WHAT ARE YOU DOING?
CLEANING MY ROOM.
WHAT?! WHY ARE YOU DOING THAT?
I LIKE TO HAVE EVERYTHING PUT AWAY AND CLEAN WHEN I GO TO SCHOOL.
IT CALMS ME DOWN AND GETS ME READY FOR THE DAY.
THEN I DOUBLE-CHECK ALL MY HOMEWORK AND MAKE SURE MY BACKPACK IS IN ORDER.
AFTER THAT, I TAKE FIVE MINUTES TO MEDITATE AND DO A POSITIVE AFFIRMATION LIKE, "YOU WILL DO YOUR BEST AT SCHOOL TODAY."
WHAT?

CAN'T YOU ACT LIKE A **NORMAL** KID?
WHAT'S **THAT** MEAN?
Y'KNOW—WAKE UP LATE, BARELY BRUSH YOUR TEETH, GET DRESSED IN A HURRY, LEAVE A MESS FOR YOUR PARENTS, AND RACE OUT THE DOOR.
BUT WHY WOULD I DO THAT WHEN THIS WAY I'M PREPARED FOR THE DAY?
DON'T YOU KNOW THE MAJOR RULE OF CHILDHOOD? WHY DO **NOW** WHAT YOU CAN PUT OFF UNTIL THE **LAST MOMENT**?
THAT DOESN'T SEEM LIKE THE **BEST** WAY TO GET AHEAD IN SCHOOL, AND MAYBE **YOU** SHOULD TRY TO ORGANIZE YOUR LIFE. IT MIGHT HELP.
I... I...
YOU KNOW WHAT?

YOU ARE A TOTAL FREAK.
MOM SAYS TO COME FOR BREAKFAST.
OKAY.
SEE WHAT I MEAN? A TOTAL MEGA-NUCLEAR DORKZILLA.
THE DOOFUS IS COMING, MOM.
PLEASE DON'T CALL YOUR BROTHER THAT.
NOW EAT YOUR BREAKFAST OR YOU'LL BE LATE.
UM... WHAT'S THIS?
BREAKFAST.
YOU HATE ME.
HEALTHY CARDBOARDY-O'S
NOW IN RUST FLAVOR
SECRET TOY SURPRISE!

ARE YOU SURE THIS IS EVEN EDIBLE?
CAN'T I JUST HAVE SOMETHING, Y'KNOW... GOOD?
GOOD?
LIKE SUGAR-FROSTED CHOCOLATE SMACKS.
JUST TRY THE CEREAL. IT'S NUTRITIOUS. BESIDES, IT HAS A TOY SURPRISE INSIDE.
WHAT KIND OF TOY?
I DON'T KNOW. THAT'S WHY THEY CALL IT A "SURPRISE."
CRUNCH

WELL...GULP... **WHATEVER** IT IS, IT'S GOTTA TASTE BETTER THAN THE CEREAL.
SCRUNCH
MILK
MOM, I CAN'T FIND THE TOY.
♫ KEEP LOOKING. ♫
NOTHING.
♫ KEEP ♫ LOOKING.
ARE YOU **SURE** IT'S IN HERE?
YES, DEAR.
FOUND IT.
THAT'S NICE, DEAR.
BUT NOW I HAVE **ANOTHER** PROBLEM.
WHAT'S THAT, DEAR?

HEALTHY CARDBOARDY-O'S
NOW IN RUST FLAVOR
SECRET TOY SURPRISE!
TOY
I'M STUCK.
OH, FOR GOODNESS SAKE! STOP FOOLING AROUND AND EAT YOUR BREAKFAST. YOU'RE GONNA BE LATE.
OKAY.
SO, WHAT WAS THE PRIZE?
HUH?
OH YEAH! UM...
RRIPP
WHAT THE–?! A **RING?!** A STUPID LOUSY DECODER RING?!
THAT'S NICE, DEAR.

SEE? DO YOU SEE? EVEN WHEN I GET A PRIZE, IT'S NOTHING I WANT!
I COULD HAVE GOTTEN ANYTHING IN THE WORLD AND I GET A USELESS RING. I MEAN— HEY, WHAT'S THIS?
UGH. EVEN BETTER... THE RING COMES WITH A POEM.
DREAM UPON THIS RING, PLEASE DO.
GIVE IT A TWIST AND IT'S SURE TO COME TRUE.
ENJOY THE WISH WITH NO REGRET,
ANYONE NEAR WILL SOON FORGET.
HEALTHY CARD BOARD O'S

OH, **COME ON!**
BUNCHA NONSENSE.
WHAT'S IN YOUR HAND?
WHAT? OH...UH... **NOTHING!**
OKAY, GUYS. THE BUS IS HERE.
TIME FOR SCHOOL.
JUST DON'T SIT NEXT TO ME ON THE BUS.
SCHOOLBUS
DON'T SIT NEXT TO ME.
DON'T SIT NEXT TO ME.

HEY! YOU SAT NEXT TO ME!
WHY DON'T YOU WANT ME SITTING NEXT TO YOU?
BECAUSE...
...BECAUSE I DON'T WANT ANYONE TO KNOW I'M RELATED TO YOU.
BUT WE'RE TWINS.
IDENTICAL TWINS.
SCHOOL BUS
WHATEVER.
JUST STOP LOOKING LIKE ME, OKAY?

OKAY. THIS IS MY SCHOOL, OR AS I CALL IT—THE FUN PREVENTION CENTER.
BOOOOOOOORING.
EVERY DAY IT'S THE SAME THING.
MS. DRONING KEEPS TALKING AND TALKING AND **TALKING** UNTIL I TOTALLY ZONE OUT...
... AND I END UP DAYDREAMING ABOUT BEING IN MY FAVORITE VIDEO GAME.
COSMIC COMMANDO!
TO BE HONEST, THIS IS THE BEST PART OF SCHOOL.
UNFORTUNATELY...

... IT NEVER LASTS.
JEREMY!
HUH?
YOU DIDN'T HEAR A WORD I'VE SAID, YOUNG MAN!
YOU BETTER START—
RIIINNGGG!
SORRY, MS. DRONING. RECESS!
SIGH
I DON'T GET PAID ENOUGH FOR THIS.

HEY, JEREMY, WHAT ARE YOU DOING? WANT TO PLAY?
NO! I'M VERY BUSY!
YOU'RE NOT DOING ANYTHING, ARE YOU?
=SIGH=
NO.

GAH! THERE IS NEVER ANYTHING TO DO!
I NEVER GET ANYTHING I WANT! I NEVER GET TO DO ANYTHING!
JUST ONCE I WISH SOMETHING WOULD HAPPEN!
POW!
WH— WHAT WAS THAT?
A BIG PROBLEM—THE BIGGEST BULLY IN SCHOOL...

...CODY SMALLS.
HAW! NICE CATCH, DUMMY!
WHAT DID YOU SAY TO ME?!
DON'T GET SHORT WITH ME, SMALLS.
YOU SAYING I'M SHORT? YOU BETTER WATCH IT!
NO. I UH...
I AM NOT SHORT, YOU UNDERSTAND? I'M THE BIGGEST KID IN SCHOOL!
IF I EVER CATCH YOU CALLING ME SHORT AGAIN, I'LL–
HEY! WHAT'S THAT?

YOU'RE WEARING A RING? HOW CUTE.
GIVE IT HERE SO I CAN SHOW EVERYONE WHAT A LOSER YOU ARE.
HEY! CUT IT OUT!
ERF. GIVE IT!
MAYBE IF I JUST TWIST IT, IT'LL—
FRZZKKK!
WHAT THE HECK WAS THAT? WHAT DID YOU DO TO ME?
I-I—
I DON'T KNOW.

ERG... I DON'T FEEL SO GOOD...
WHAT WAS THAT?
I HAVE NO IDEA. BUT, UGH, I CAN'T GET THIS RING OFF.
RRIIIINNGG
COME ON. RECESS IS OVER.
I KNOW, I KNOW... AND WILL YOU STOP LOOKING LIKE ME?
WELL, YOU SURE TOOK CARE OF CODY.
YEAH, BUT I HAVE NO CLUE **WHAT** I DID. I THINK IT WAS THIS RING.
UH... I THINK I KNOW WHAT THAT RING DID TO CODY.
WHATEVER IT WAS, I DON'T THINK IT WAS ANY–

RAAWWRR!
—BIG DEAL.

WHAT KIND OF RING IS THAT?
IT'S SUPPOSED TO GRANT WISHES!
CODY MUST HAVE WISHED TO BE BIG!
YOU HAVE TO FIX THIS! SOMEONE'S GOING TO GET HURT!
ME? NO WAY! HOW AM I SUPPOSED TO STOP HIM?
MAYBE WITH YOUR NEW OUTFIT.
MY WHAT?

GAH! WHERE DID THIS COME FROM?
TELL ME YOU WOULDN'T FREAK OUT IF A COSTUME JUST APPEARED ON YOU.
I KNOW JUSTIN WOULD.
I'M FREAKING OUT! IS THAT REAL?!
HOW SHOULD I KNOW IF IT'S REAL?
WELL, TRY IT OUT.
KLIK
WHOA!
KLIK KLAK
PHEW! I WAS AFRAID THAT WOULD-

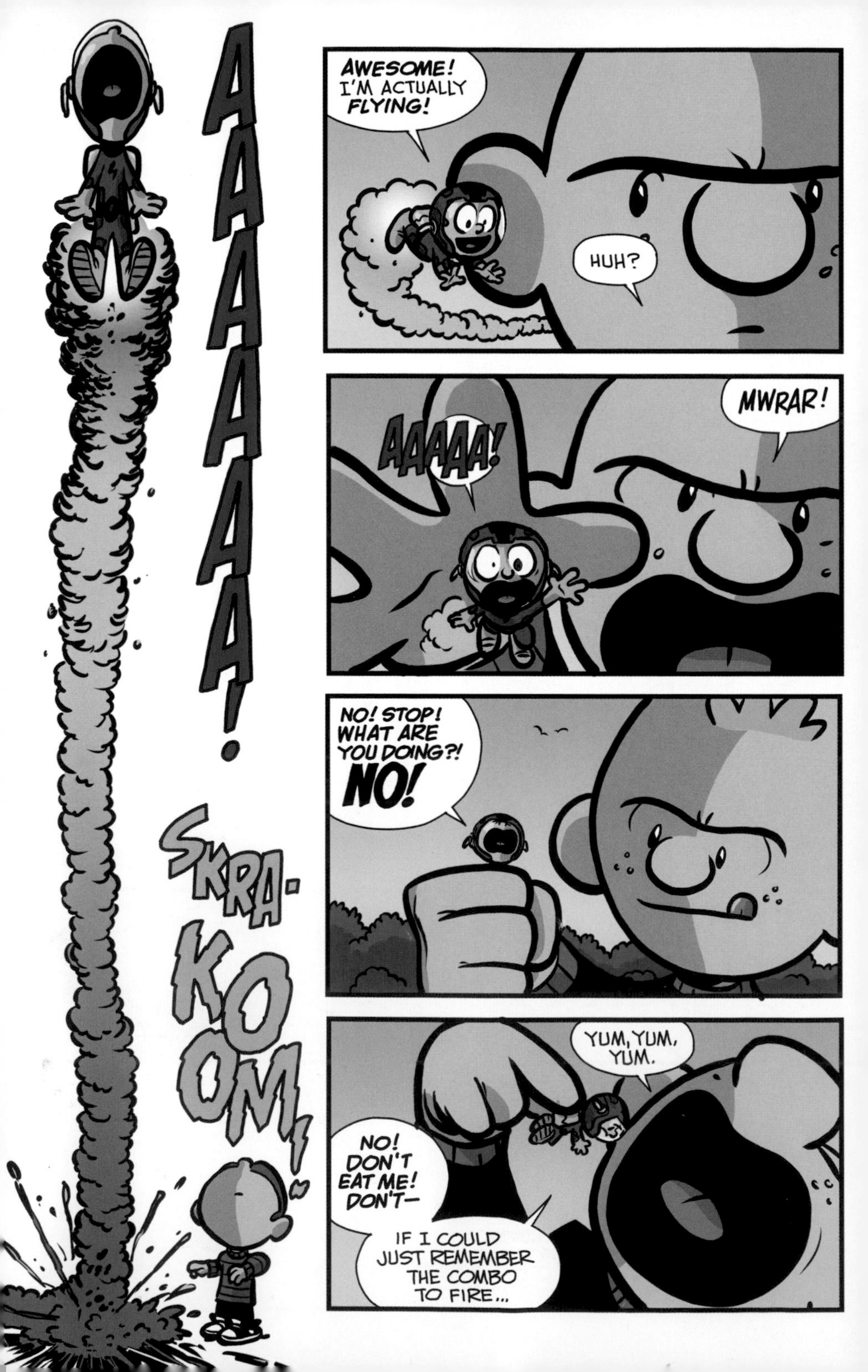
AAAAAAAA!
SKRA-KOOM!
AWESOME! I'M ACTUALLY FLYING!
HUH?
MWRAR!
AAAAA!
NO! STOP! WHAT ARE YOU DOING?! NO!
YUM, YUM, YUM.
NO! DON'T EAT ME! DON'T—
IF I COULD JUST REMEMBER THE COMBO TO FIRE...

HOW 'BOUT YOU EAT LASERS INSTEAD OF ME?
ERK.
BZAAP!
HEY! I HIT THE RIGHT COMBO AND THE SUIT FIRED JUST LIKE IN THE VIDEO GAME!
COOL!
ALL I HAVE TO DO IS HIT THE RIGHT COMBOS TO DO SPECIAL MOVES!
GAME ON!
AW, MAN. I BETTER FIGURE OUT A WAY TO STOP CODY BEFORE HE DESTROYS THE WHOLE SCHOOL.
HMMMMM, THEN AGAIN, NO MORE SCHOOL SOUNDS NICE.

YOU BETTER SAVE THE SCHOOL. MOM WILL NOT BE HAPPY IF YOU DON'T!
WHEN IS MOM EVER HAPPY?
=SIGH= YEAH, OKAY.
HMM. IN THE VIDEO GAME, THE COSMIC COMMANDO HAS A SHRINK RAY.
WHAT WAS THE COMBO AGAIN?
UP-DOWN-A-A-B-DOWN?
SKROOM!

RAAWWRRR!
MAYBE IT WAS UP-DOWN-A-A-B-UP?
SWIPE!
WHOA!
YIKES! GOTTA GET AWAY!
GOTTA GET HIGHER!
UP-DOWN-A-A-B-A?

FWASH!

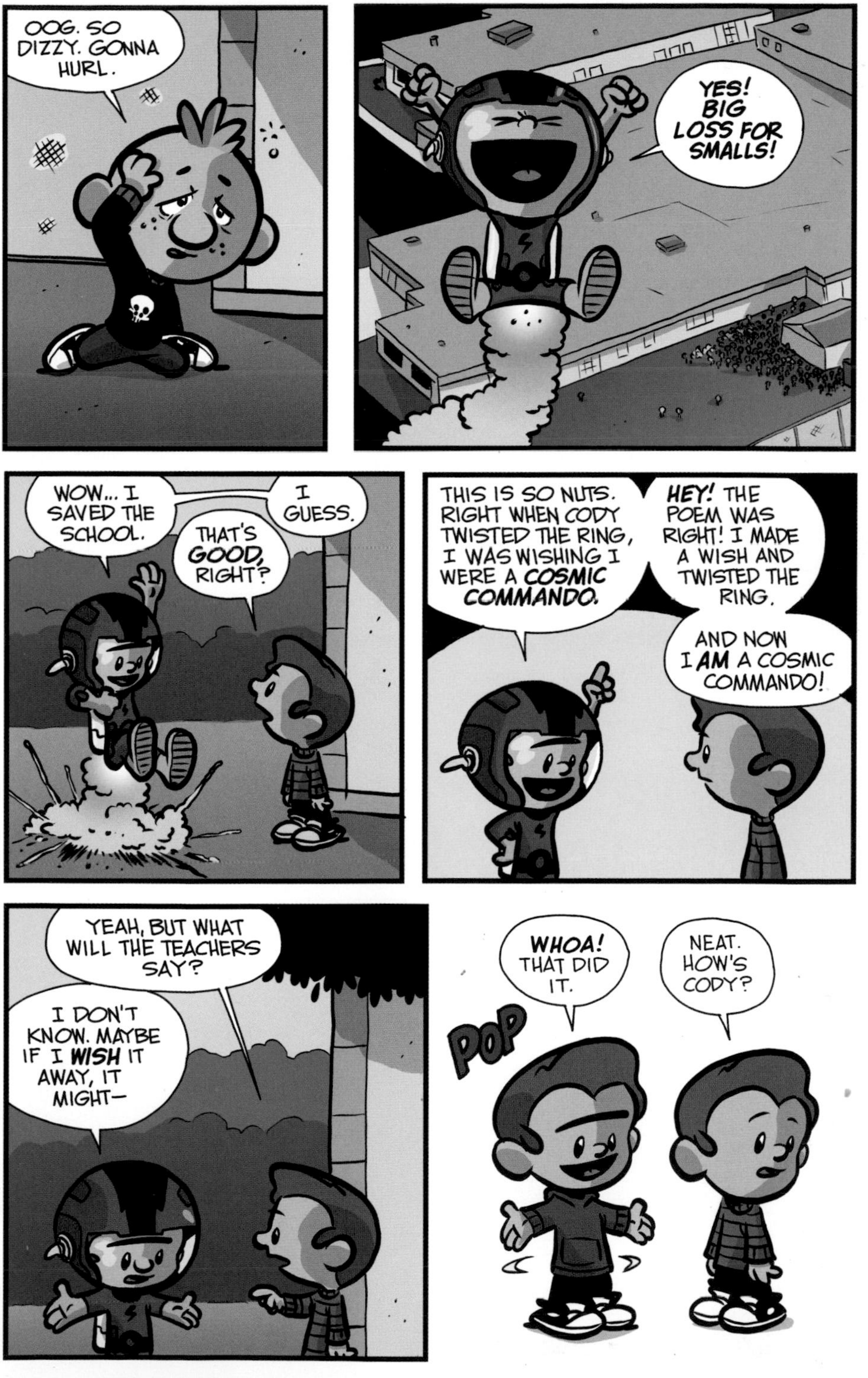

OOG. SO DIZZY. GONNA HURL.
YES! BIG LOSS FOR SMALLS!
WOW... I SAVED THE SCHOOL.
I GUESS.
THAT'S GOOD, RIGHT?
THIS IS SO NUTS. RIGHT WHEN CODY TWISTED THE RING, I WAS WISHING I WERE A COSMIC COMMANDO.
HEY! THE POEM WAS RIGHT! I MADE A WISH AND TWISTED THE RING.
AND NOW I AM A COSMIC COMMANDO!
YEAH, BUT WHAT WILL THE TEACHERS SAY?
I DON'T KNOW. MAYBE IF I WISH IT AWAY, IT MIGHT—
POP
WHOA! THAT DID IT.
NEAT. HOW'S CODY?

DOES CODY LOOK **SMALLER** TO YOU?
UM...DIDN'T NOTICE.
ISN'T IT WEIRD? NO ONE IN THE SCHOOL SEEMS TO BE FREAKED OUT BY HOW ***HUGE*** CODY WAS.
MAYBE THE WISH YOU MADE ALSO TOOK AWAY EVERYONE'S ***MEMORY.***
WHAT ARE YOU GOING TO DO NOW?
GO TO CLASS, GENIUS. DUH! THE BELL RANG.

JEREMY, WAIT A MINUTE!
WHAT NOW?
I WAS JUST THINKING ABOUT THE RING.
I TOLD YOU— I CAN'T TAKE IT OFF.
NO. NO. I WAS JUST WONDERING...
YOU TWISTED IT AND IT GAVE YOU YOUR WISH.
YEAH. I GOT THAT.
SO, WHY CAN'T YOU TWIST IT AGAIN AND GET ANOTHER WISH?
BLINK BLINK
I WISH I DIDN'T HAVE A BROTHER.
TWIST TWIST TWIST

RATS!
GUESS YOU ONLY GET ONE WISH PER PERSON.
GUESS SO.
SAY... DO YOU THINK I COULD–
NO!
AND STOP LOOKING LIKE ME.

CHAPTER TWO

BROTHERLY SHOVE

I MEAN, MY LIFE IS PRETTY GREAT.
I HAVE MY BOOKS, OLD MOVIES, AND RETRO VIDEO GAMES.
MY PARENTS ARE COOL. SCHOOL IS GOOD.
IN FACT, I'M REALLY HAPPY AND LIFE COULDN'T BE BETTER.
WELL, EXCEPT FOR ONE LITTLE THING...

...MY TWIN BROTHER, JEREMY.
I TRY TO BE FRIENDS WITH HIM, BUT HE'S ALWAYS JUST MEAN.
HE'S A KNOW-IT-ALL. THINKS HE'S BETTER THAN EVERYONE ELSE.
WHEN I ASK TO PLAY WITH ONE OF HIS TOYS, HE ALWAYS SAYS NO...
...BUT WHEN HE WANTS TO PLAY WITH ONE OF MINE... WELL...

...THIS HAPPENS.
GIVE ME THE TOY NOOOW!
HE'S ANTI-SOCIAL...
LEAVE ME ALONE!
...THOUGHTLESS...
SO WHAT IF I BROKE YOUR TOY?
MINE'S JUST FINE.
SUCKER.
...SELFISH...
SO? I ATE IT ALL.
YOU'LL HAVE ANOTHER BIRTHDAY CAKE NEXT YEAR.
...AND LAZY.
WHILE YOU'RE UP, CAN YOU GO TO THE STORE, GET ME JELLY BEANS, BRING THEM HOME, AND FEED THEM TO ME?

HE ALWAYS TRIES TO GET ME TO DO HIS HOMEWORK FOR HIM...
... HIS CHORES...
YOU NEVER TAKE OUT THE GARBAGE.
... REALLY, ANYTHING HE DOESN'T WANT TO DO.
EAT MY SPINACH.
HONESTLY, THE ONLY THING JEREMY REALLY CARES ABOUT IS... JEREMY.
ALL I REALLY WANT IS TO BE HIS FRIEND. AND NOW THAT HE HAS THAT RING AND THAT SUIT, HE'LL NEVER HAVE TIME FOR ME.
SNIFF

CHAPTER THREE

TAKEOFF!

BRIIING!
WHERE'S JEREMY?
HE'S ALWAYS LATE AND— OH!
YOU NEED TO BE ON TIME MORE!
HEY! WHERE ARE YOU GOING?
AREN'T YOU TAKING THE BUS HOME?
ARE YOU KIDDING?
C'MON. IF YOU GOT A MAGIC RING THAT GAVE YOU THE POWERS OF A CHARACTER FROM YOUR FAVORITE VIDEO GAME, WHAT WOULD YOU DO?
I'M GOING OFF TO HAVE SOME FUN!
BUT WHAT ABOUT ME?

THIS IS THE COOLEST THING EVER!

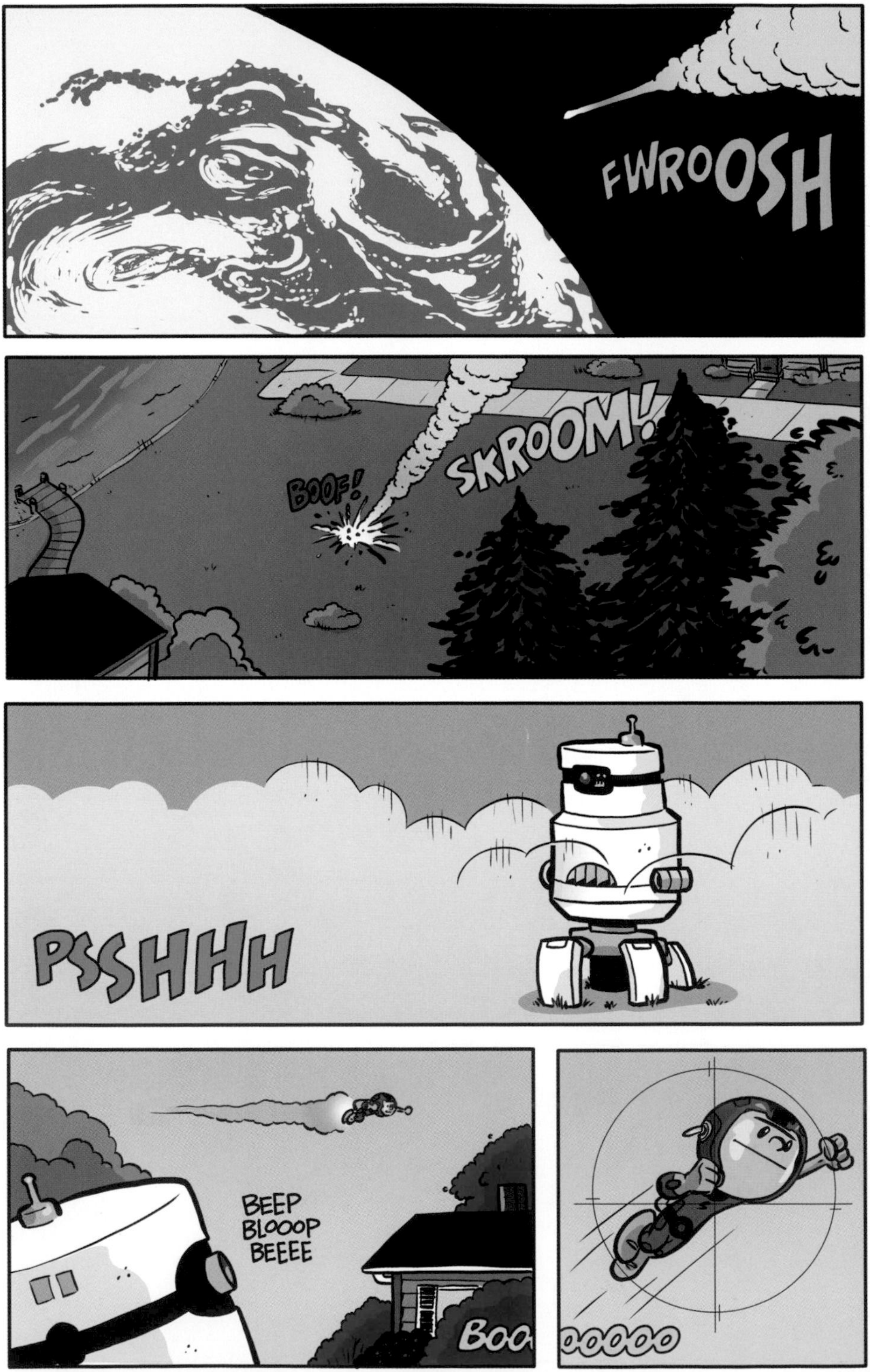
FWROOSH
BOOF!
SKROOM!
PSSHHH
BEEP
BLOOOP
BEEEE
BOOOOOOOO

WHOA!
FRZAAKKK
WHAT THE HECK IS THIS?
WAIT A MINUTE.
THIS LOOKS LIKE THE COSMIC COMMANDO ROBOT PROBE FROM THE FIRST LEVEL OF THE GAME.
IS IT REAL...
WHRRR
YEAH... REAL SCARY.

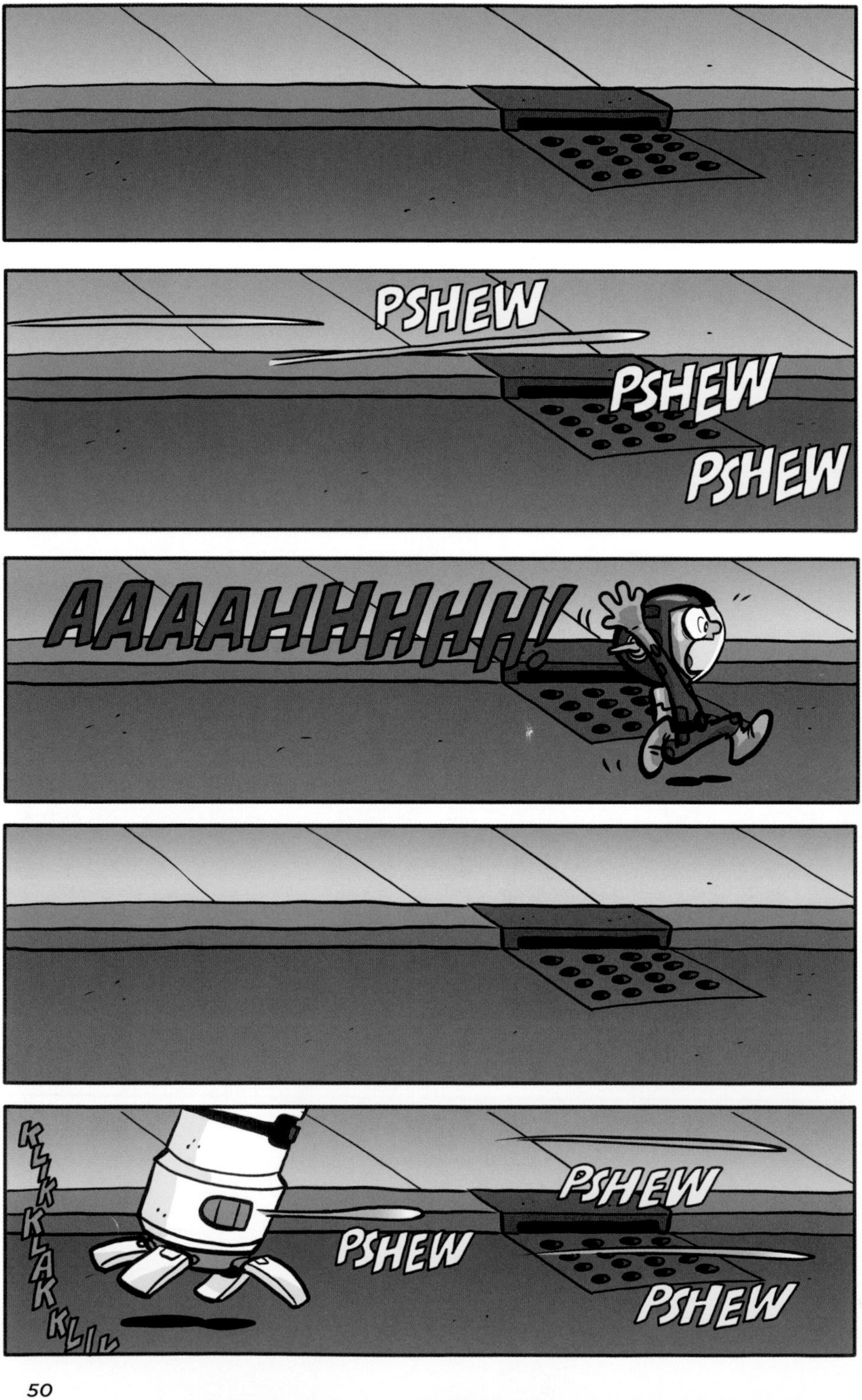
PSHEW
PSHEW
PSHEW
AAAAHHHHH!
KLIKKLAKKLI
PSHEW
PSHEW
PSHEW

≑HUFF HUFF≑ THAT THING IS REAL... AND IT'S SHOOTING AT ME.
HEY, WHERE DID IT GO? IT WAS JUST—
TARGET ACQUIRED: COSMIC COMMANDO.
VWRRR
HOW IS THE ROBOT FROM MY VIDEO GAME HERE?!
IF I WAS PLAYING THE VIDEO GAME, I COULD JUST—
OH... DUH.
RRRT

MAYBE THIS IS LIKE THE GAME. JUST HAVE TO REMEMBER HOW TO **DEFEAT** THIS THING.
A-BUTTON TO FIRE... I HOPE.
SKROOM!
ENERGY
FSHHHHH
HEY! ITS ENERGY LEVEL WENT DOWN! **AWESOME!**
GAME ON.

SKROOM!
BWOOP
ENERGY
OH, YEAH. YOU HAVE TO BLAST THE LEGS TO DEFEAT IT. THIS'LL BE EASY. ALL I HAVE TO DO IS—
SNAP
FRZAKKK
YOWTCH!
HEY! THAT REALLY HURT!
UH-OH. MY ENERGY BAR WENT DOWN, TOO. I WONDER WHAT HAPPENS WHEN IT RUNS DOWN TO ZERO?
ENERGY
GUESS I BETTER NOT FIND OUT.

THIS SHOULD BE CAKE.
JUST HAVE TO KNOCK OUT ALL ITS LEGS, AND—
ZARK!
WHOA!
BUT CAKE NEVER SHOOTS BACK!
FORGET THAT. IF I'M NOT CAREFUL, I'M GONNA END UP A PANCAKE.
SHOULD BE EASY AS...
...ONE...
THROOM!
... TWO...
SHOOM!
... THREE!
FZARKK!

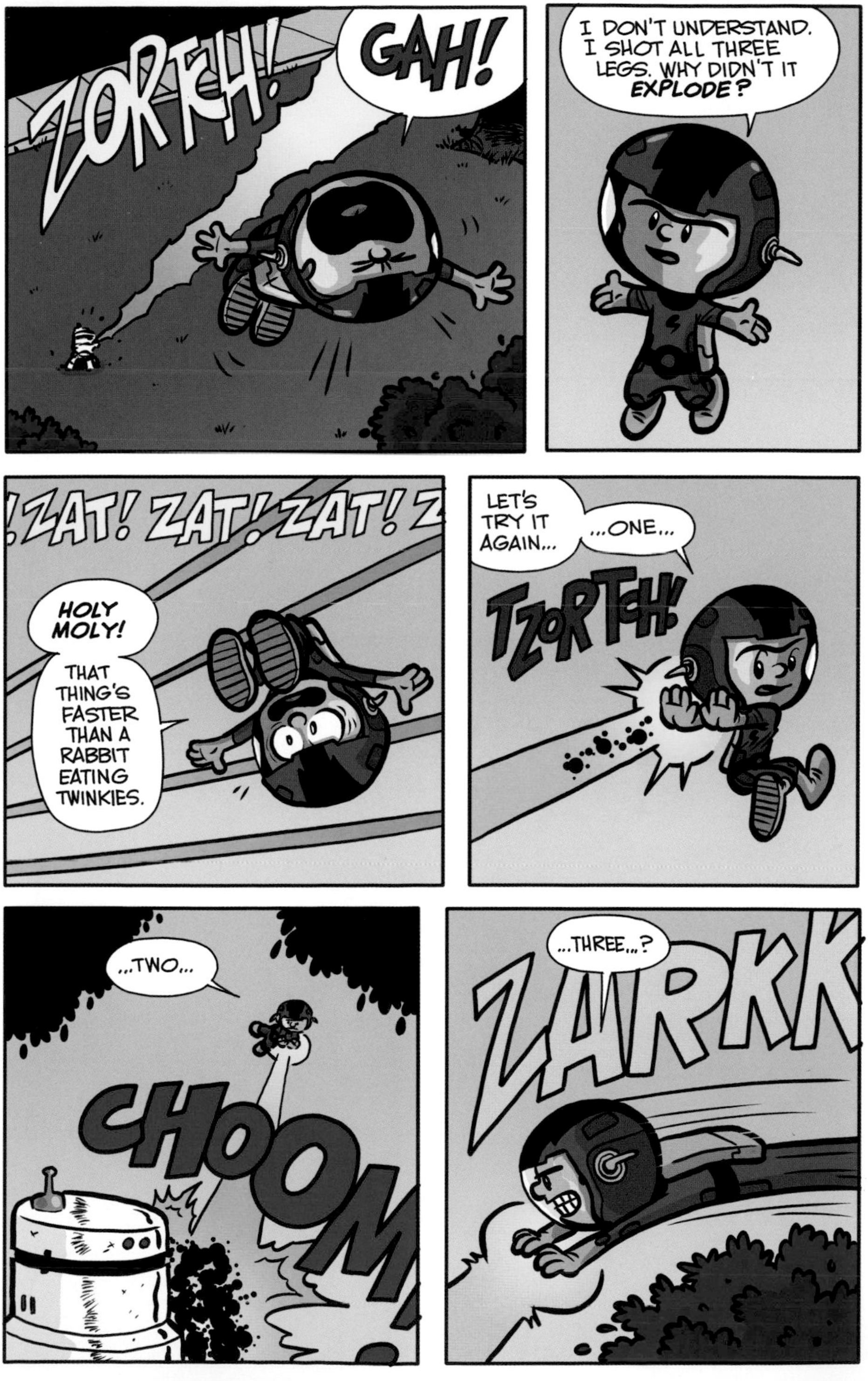
ZORTCH!
GAH!
I DON'T UNDERSTAND. I SHOT ALL THREE LEGS. WHY DIDN'T IT EXPLODE?
ZAT! ZAT! ZAT!
HOLY MOLY!
THAT THING'S FASTER THAN A RABBIT EATING TWINKIES.
LET'S TRY IT AGAIN...
...ONE...
TZORTCH!
...TWO...
CHOOM!
...THREE...?
ZARKK

NOTHING AGAIN.
ENERGY
WHAT AM I DOING WRONG?
WAIT! I KNOW! I JUST-
ZORTCH!
AAGHH!
SPLOOSH!

HMM.
THE SUIT WORKS UNDER-WATER.
THAT'S GOOD TO KNOW.
ENERGY
BUT... OUCH.
THAT **REALLY** HURTS.
I FIGURED IT OUT, THOUGH.
IT'S LIKE **JUSTIN** ALWAYS SAYS...
...I NEED TO BE **ON TIME.**
YEAH. DON'T TELL JUSTIN I ACTUALLY LISTEN TO HIM.
ALL I NEED TO DO IS HIT ALL THREE LEGS AT THE SAME TIME.

THAT MEANS I HAVE TO GET IN CLOSE...
ZAP! ZAP! ZAP! ZAP! ZAP!
...WHICH ALSO MEANS IT FIRES MORE AT ME!
JUST GOTTA GET INTO THE RIGHT SPOT AND...

SKRAKKADOOM!

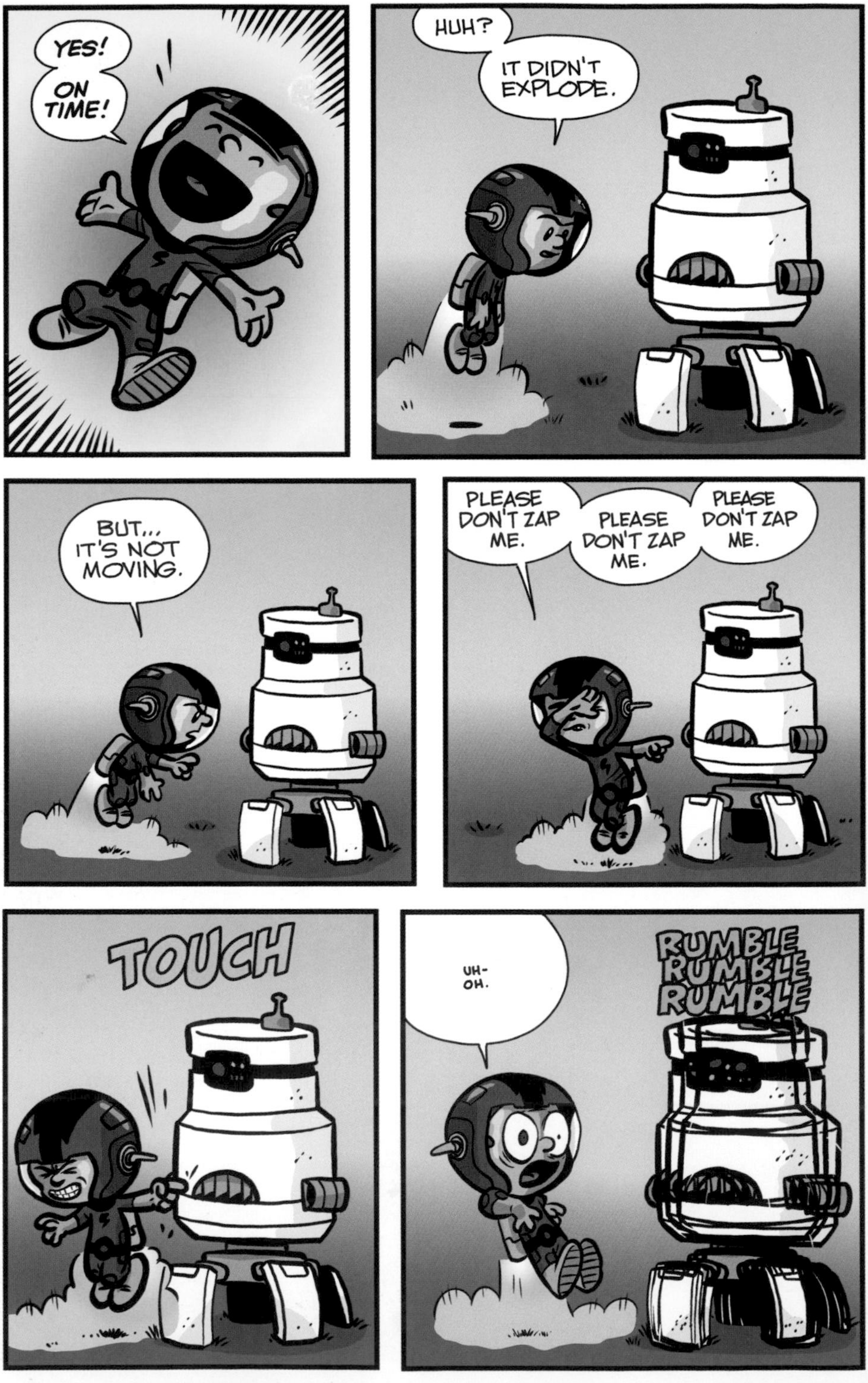
YES!
ON TIME!
HUH?
IT DIDN'T EXPLODE.
BUT... IT'S NOT MOVING.
PLEASE DON'T ZAP ME.
PLEASE DON'T ZAP ME.
PLEASE DON'T ZAP ME.
TOUCH
UH-OH.
RUMBLE RUMBLE RUMBLE

CRUMBLE
!
HEY!
WHADDYA KNOW?
I BEAT IT!
FADE
WHOA.
UM... I BETTER GET HOME.

CUTSCENE

SKORN!

I THOUGHT I DISPOSED OF THEIR ROTTEN CORPS YEARS AGO.
APPARENTLY I WAS **MISTAKEN.**
IT SEEMS I, **SKORN,** HAVE **ANOTHER** BUG TO SQUASH...
...AND, LIKE ALL THE **PREVIOUS** COMMANDOS, THEIR FAMILY AND FRIENDS AS WELL.
CLICK
HAHAHAHAHAHAHAHAHA!

CHAPTER FOUR

BIG TIME!

SIGH
FWASH!
HEY!
WAIT UP!

JEREMY! WHERE ARE YOU GOING?
QUIET! I HAVE TO PLAY MY VIDEO GAME!
WHY? WHAT HAPPENED?
NOTHING! LEAVE ME ALONE!
BUT... DON'T YOU HAVE HOMEWORK?
JUST GET OUT OF MY ROOM!
AND STOP LOOKING LIKE ME!
SLAM!

THUMP
EVERYTHING YOU NEED TO KNOW!
1
COSMIC COMMANDO TIPS & TRICKS TO BEAT EVERY LEVEL!

PREPARE FOR DEFEAT, COMMANDO!
TARGET ACQUIRED.
POWER LOSS!
JEREMY! DINNER!

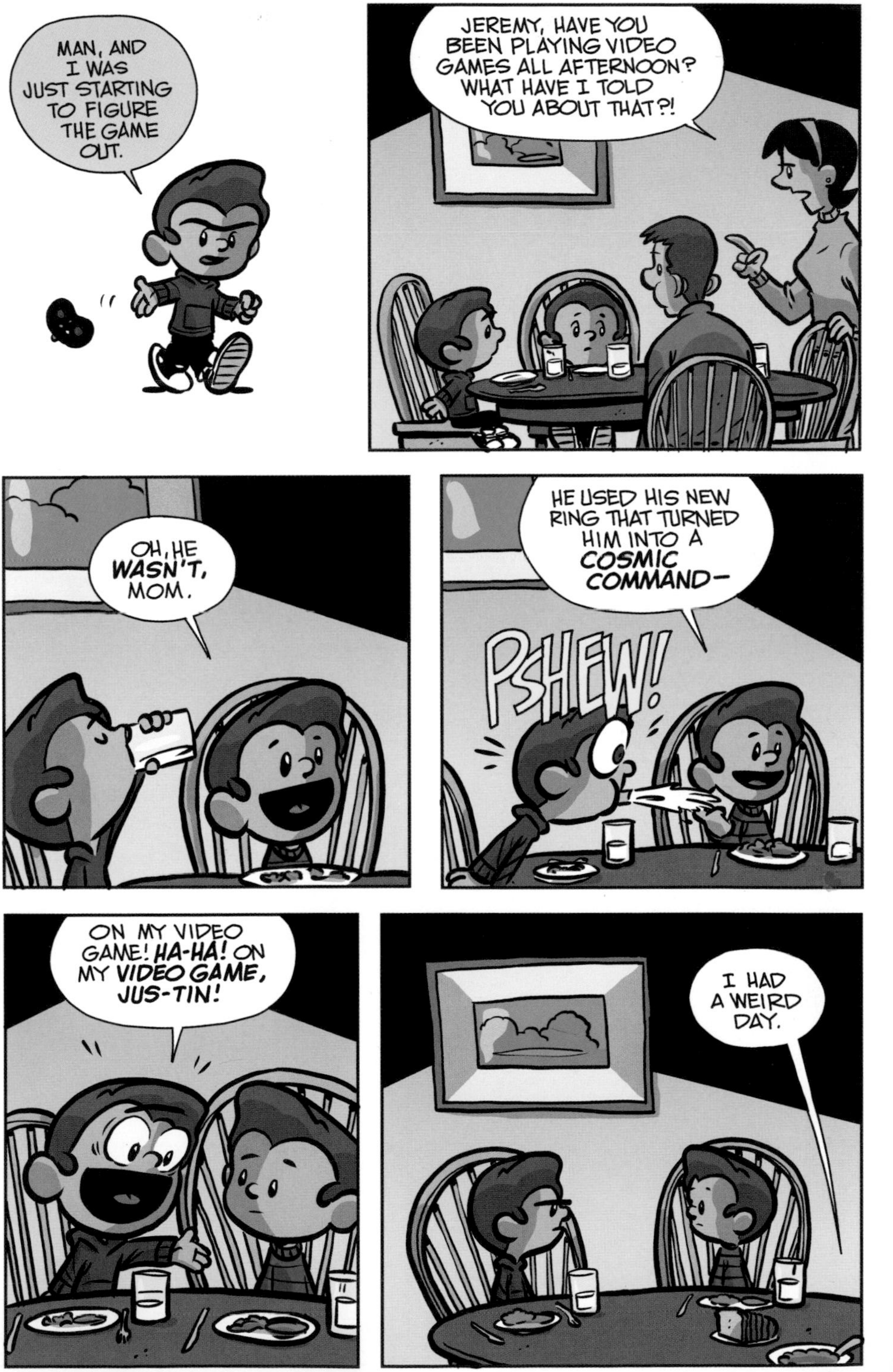
MAN, AND I WAS JUST STARTING TO FIGURE THE GAME OUT.
JEREMY, HAVE YOU BEEN PLAYING VIDEO GAMES ALL AFTERNOON? WHAT HAVE I TOLD YOU ABOUT THAT?!
OH, HE WASN'T, MOM.
HE USED HIS NEW RING THAT TURNED HIM INTO A COSMIC COMMAND—
PSHEW!
ON MY VIDEO GAME! HA-HA! ON MY VIDEO GAME, JUS-TIN!
I HAD A WEIRD DAY.

I THOUGHT I SAW A METEORITE CRASH NEARBY. THEN I THOUGHT I SAW A LITTLE MAN IN ARMOR FIGHTING A ROBOT.
BUT I FEEL LIKE I'M STARTING TO FORGET IT.
YOU KNOW WHAT THAT MEANS.
I MUST BE OVERDUE FOR AN EYE EXAM.
PHEW!
SCARF
CHEW SCARF MUNCH
MUNCH
CHOMP
CHEW
I'MDONECANIBEEXCUSEDTHANKYOU.
HEY! WAIT UP!

WHAT **REALLY** HAPPENED TODAY?! DID YOU FIGHT A ROBOT?!
YES.
A **SMALL** ONE.
THE ONE FROM THE FIRST LEVEL OF COSMIC COMMANDO.
WAIT. ARE YOU SAYING THE VIDEO GAME IS PLAYING OUT IN **REAL LIFE?**
SEEMS LIKE IT.
DON'T YOU THINK YOU SHOULD TELL MOM AND DAD?
ARE YOU NUTS? THEY'D **NEVER** BELIEVE ME.
BESIDES, ALL I HAVE TO DO IS FIGURE OUT THE GAME AND I'LL BE ABLE TO **DEFEAT** IT IN REAL LIFE.
BUT...

...MAYBE I SHOULD HELP YOU. I'VE BEEN READING ABOUT THE GAME AND I–
YOU?!
ARE YOU KIDDING? YOU'RE AWFUL AT VIDEO GAMES!
GO READ THE BOOK AND LEAVE THE REAL WORK TO PEOPLE WHO ACTUALLY KNOW HOW TO PLAY.
OH, AND–
I KNOW...
STOP LOOKING LIKE YOU.

THE NEXT MORNING...
JEREMY! TIME TO GET UP!
UGH.
YOU LOOK EXHAUSTED, SWEETIE. YOU BETTER NOT HAVE BEEN UP LATE PLAYING VIDEO GAMES.
UH... NO, NO! I WAS... UM —
DOING HOMEWORK.
OH, UH, YEAH. HOMEWORK.
COME ON. THE BUS IS HERE.
YOU DID DO IT, RIGHT?
OH, YEAH. SURE.

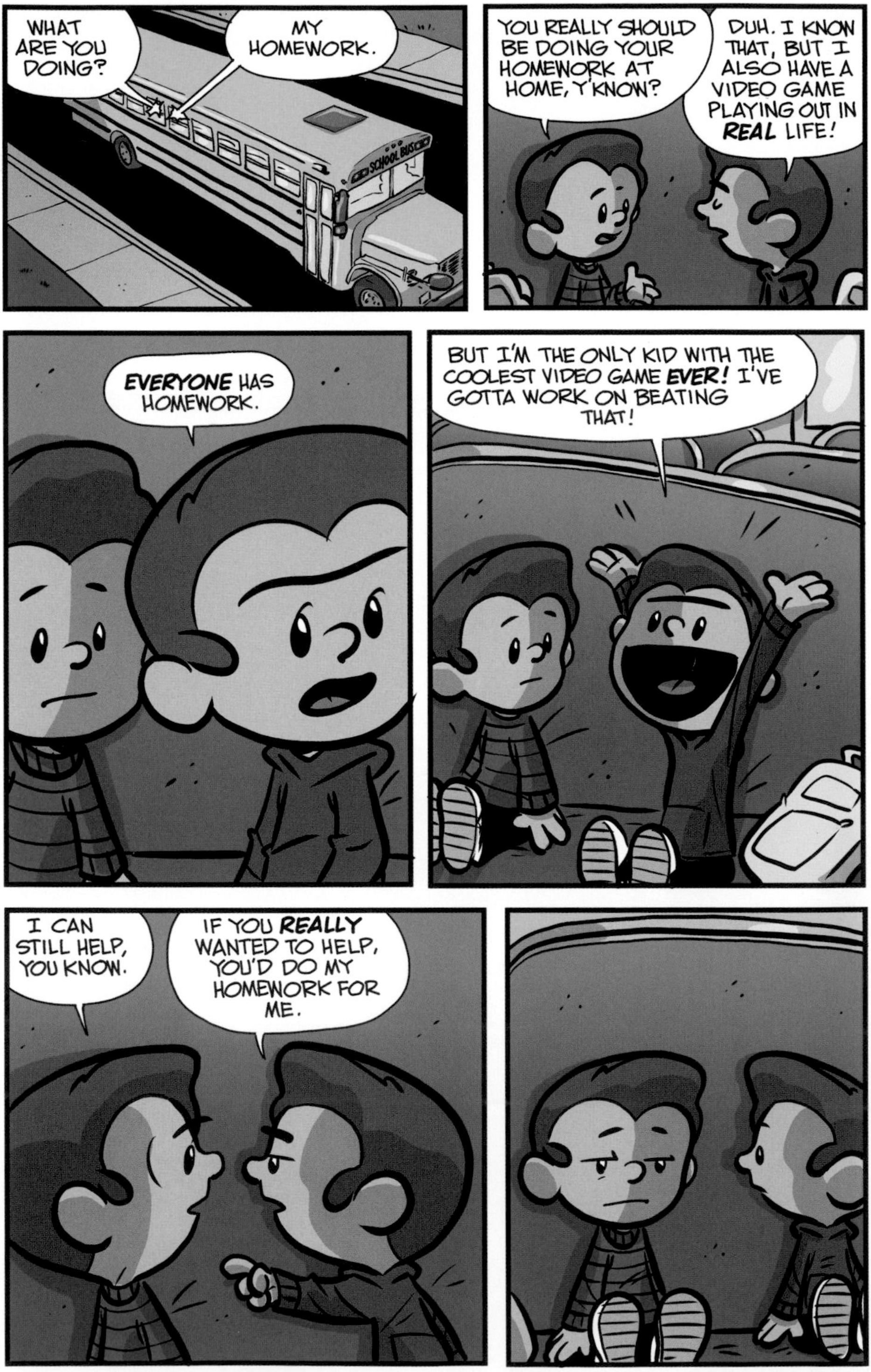
WHAT ARE YOU DOING?
MY HOMEWORK.
YOU REALLY SHOULD BE DOING YOUR HOMEWORK AT HOME, Y'KNOW?
DUH. I KNOW THAT, BUT I ALSO HAVE A VIDEO GAME PLAYING OUT IN **REAL** LIFE!
EVERYONE HAS HOMEWORK.
BUT I'M THE ONLY KID WITH THE COOLEST VIDEO GAME **EVER!** I'VE GOTTA WORK ON BEATING THAT!
I CAN STILL HELP, YOU KNOW.
IF YOU **REALLY** WANTED TO HELP, YOU'D DO MY HOMEWORK FOR ME.

FORGET IT.
BUT DID PLAYING THE VIDEO GAME AT HOME HELP?
OF COURSE.
I'M HAVING TROUBLE ON THE SECOND LEVEL, THOUGH.
WELL, I'VE BEEN READING THE "COSMIC COMMANDO TIPS AND TRICKS" BOOK, AND THE GAME CAUSES A LOT OF DESTRUCTION.
SO? IT'S JUST A GAME.
YEAH, BUT WHAT IF THIS REAL VIDEO GAME DOES SOME REAL DAMAGE?
SCHOOL
EVEN IF YOU BEAT THE GAME'S FINAL LEVEL, WILL THE REAL DAMAGE BE REPAIRED?
SCHOOL
SPEAKING OF WHICH... YOU KNOW WHAT THE NEXT LEVEL IS, RIGHT?
IT'S THE—

CHOOM!
– GIANT ROBOT LEVEL.
WELL, YOU BETTER SUIT UP AND–
– GO.

WHOA.
WHOA.
WHAT ARE YOU DOING?
ZORT!
WHAT'S IT LOOK LIKE?
TRYING TO BEAT THIS ROBOT!
FRZAAAP!
THERE'S AN EASIER WAY!
WAIT, WHAT?
THRUOOM!

I READ IT IN THE TIPS AND TRICKS BOOK.
THE WHAT?!
THE BOOK YOU THREW AT ME.
WHATEVER.
YIKES!
SWAT!
YOU WANT TO TELL ME WHAT THE EASY WAY IS?!
YOU JUST NEED TO PRESS THE BUTTON ON THE LEFT SIDE OF HIS HEAD!
OH... IS THAT ALL?

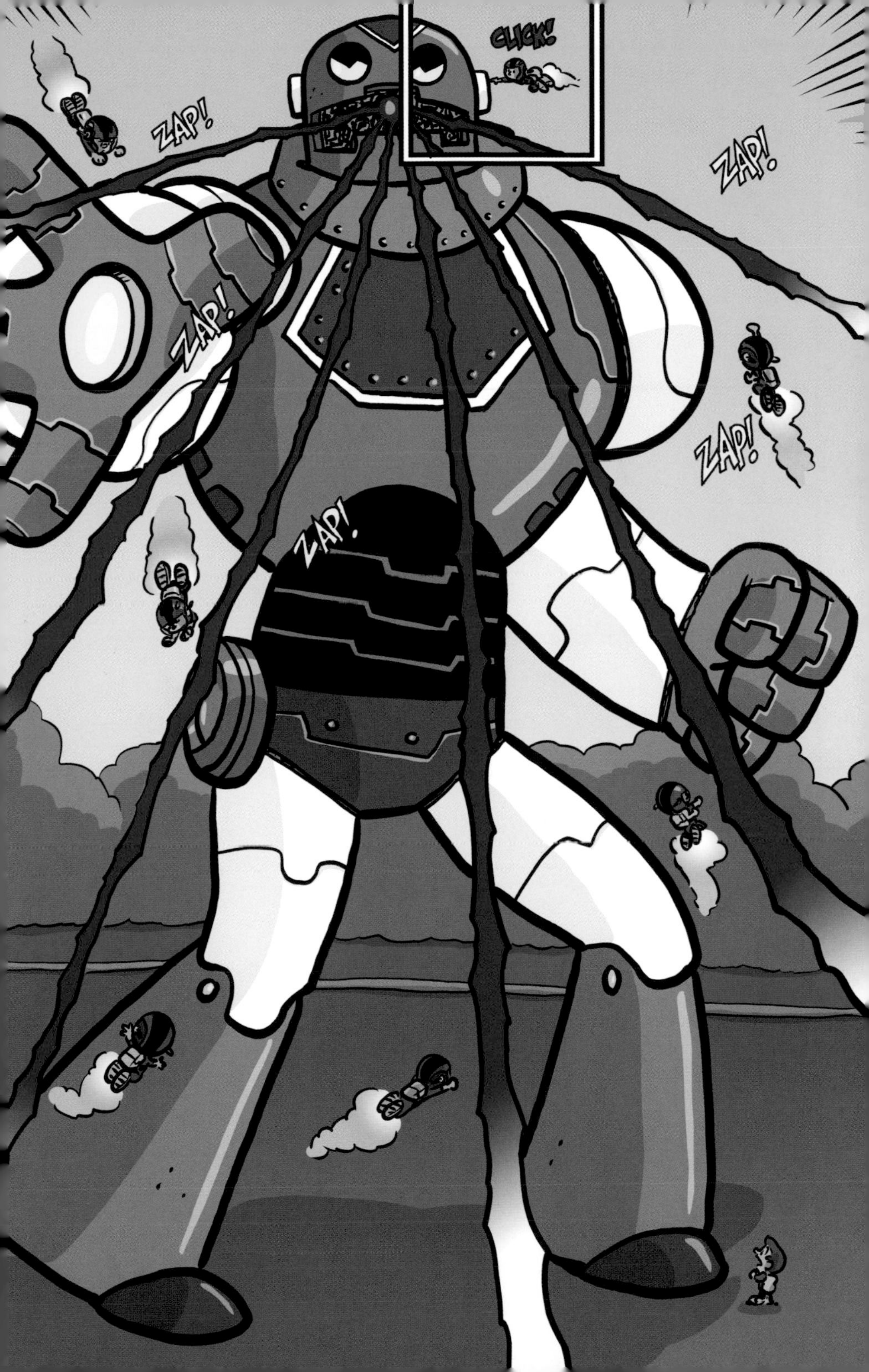

CLICK!
ZAP!
ZAP!
ZAP!
ZAP!
ZAP!

BEEWOOOP!
WOW! THAT WAS SO COOL! IT JUST IMPLODED!
ALL THANKS TO ME, RIGHT?
YOU?! I HAD TO DODGE AND WEAVE THROUGH LASER FIRE! WHAT DID YOU DO?!
I TOLD YOU THE TRICK TO BEAT-
RING!
WHATEVER. C'MON, WE'RE LATE.

JEREMY?!
WHAT?
JEREMY?!
WHAT?!
WAIT UP!
ISN'T IT WEIRD THAT NO ONE EVEN SEEMS TO BE AWARE THAT A GIANT ROBOT WAS OUTSIDE THE SCHOOL?
IT'S BECAUSE OF THE RING.
I GET THAT. I'M JUST WONDERING—
LOOK. I HAVE TO GET TO CLASS AND I DON'T WANT TO HEAR MS. DRONING SAY, "YOU'RE LATE AGAIN, JEREMY."
I WAS JUST THINKING THAT MAYBE THE TIPS BOOK MIGHT **EXPLAIN** WHAT IS HAP—
I DON'T NEED IT.
BUT IT REALLY—

JUSTIN, I HAVE **NEVER** READ AN INSTRUCTION BOOK. I DON'T NEED TO.
MAYBE **YOU** NEED TO READ THE GUIDEBOOKS, BUT I FIGURE THINGS OUT BY **DOING** THEM.
ONCE I FIGURE IT OUT, IT'S CAKE.
READING ABOUT CLIMBING MOUNT EVEREST IS NOTHING LIKE **REALLY** CLIMBING IT.
BUT NOBODY CLIMBS MOUNT EVEREST WITHOUT STUDYING THE PROCESS FIRST. JUST LIKE DOING HOMEWORK HELPS YOU **UNDERSTAND** THINGS WHEN YOU TAKE A TEST.
I'LL BE FINE.
NOW, I HAVE TO GET TO CLASS **BEFORE** MS. DRONING–
JEREMY! YOU COULD GET HURT!

THIS IS DANGEROUS STUFF. YOU NEED TO BE PREPARED OR YOU COULD REALLY GET HURT.
IT'S A GAME, JUSTIN.
I MEAN, IT'S A REAL-LIFE GAME, BUT IT'S JUST A GAME!
I CAN HANDLE IT.
I GET THAT YOU'RE WORRIED, BUT I'M FINE.
YOU WANT TO READ THE BOOK? BE MY GUEST, I DON'T NEED IT.
BUT, JEREMY-
ENOUGH! I DON'T WANT TO HEAR MS. DRONING SAY-
YOU'RE LATE AGAIN, JEREMY!

C'MON. INTO CLASS.
YES, MS. DRONING.
SEE YOU LATER, JEREMY!
I DON'T KNOW WHAT THE BIG DEAL IS ABOUT READING.
I MEAN, I DO JUST FINE WITHOUT READING AHEAD. I'VE DEFEATED TWO ROBOTS AS WELL AS CODY SMALLS.
AND NOTHING WENT WRONG WITH THAT.
OUT OF THE WAY, PIPSQUEAK!
=AHEM= ANYWAY, WHAT GOOD WILL READING OR STUDYING DO FOR ME ANYWAY?
OKAY, CLASS. TIME FOR A QUIZ ON LAST NIGHT'S READING LESSON.

CUTSCENE

SKORN!

MY FAVORITE ROBOT!
THAT COMMANDO IS CONNIVING! HOW DID HE KNOW OF MY SECRET SELF-DESTRUCTION SWITCH?!
I WILL DESTROY HIM AND ESCAPE THIS DIGITAL PRISON!
FOR TOO LONG HAVE I BEEN TRAPPED IN WHAT THE EARTHERS CALL A "VIDEO GAME."
WHAM!
I WILL DO WHATEVER IT TAKES TO DEFEAT THIS COMMANDO AND WIN MY FREEDOM!
NOW I HAVE SOMETHING SPECIAL PLANNED.

CHAPTER FIVE

LEVELING UP

JEREMY!
OH, JEREMY!
ALMOST GOT AWAY.
YES, MS. DRONING?
I WANT TO TALK TO YOU ABOUT YOUR EFFORT IN CLASS.
YOU SEEM DISTRACTED LATELY.
I JUST DON'T UNDERSTAND. YOUR BROTHER IS SO ENGAGED IN CLASS. HE ALWAYS GETS HIS HOMEWORK DONE. HE'S A JOY. BUT YOU'RE... YOU'RE...
NOT TRYING VERY HARD.
I GET IT.
JEREMY, YOU'RE A GOOD KID. YOU JUST NEED TO WORK HARDER.
YOU NEED TO BE...
DON'T SAY IT.
...MORE LIKE YOUR BROTHER.
I- I-

FINE, MS. DRONING. I'LL TRY.
I'M GLAD TO HEAR YOU SAY THAT.
EVERYONE ALWAYS COMPARES ME TO JUSTIN.
IT'S SO MEANTASTIC.
"JUSTIN IS SO NICE."
"JUSTIN WORKS SO HARD."
"WHY CAN'T YOU BE MORE LIKE JUSTIN?"
IT'S HARD ENOUGH BEING **JEREMY**.
HOW AM I SUPPOSED TO BE MORE LIKE **HIM**?
AND WHY WOULD I WANT TO?

HA HA HA HA HA! JUSTIN, YOU'RE SO FUNNY!
AHEM
OH, NOT REALLY.
WHAT ARE YOU DOING AFTER SCHOOL?
AHEM
OH, HOMEWORK. THE USUAL.
DO YOU WANT TO HANG OUT? MAYBE AFTER–
AHEM!
COME ON, JUSTIN. LET'S GO HOME.

SEE YOU GUYS LATER.
WHY'S JUSTIN'S BROTHER SO *MEAN*?
HI, JUSTIN.
HI, ANNA.
CAN'T TALK.
HAVE TO GO.
OH, UM... **SORRY,** ANNA. SEE YOU TOMORROW.
WHAT'S YOUR PROBLEM, JEREMY?

MY PROBLEM? MY PROBLEM?!
I'M FIGHTING FOR MY LIFE HERE AND IT'S SOCIAL HOUR FOR YOU!
I THOUGHT YOU DIDN'T NEED MY HELP.
I—I DON'T.
ACTUALLY, YOU DO.
THE TIPS BOOK SAYS THE NEXT LEVEL IS—
I KNOW WHAT THE NEXT LEVEL IS AND--
HI, JUSTIN!
HI!
GRRRRR.

I'M GOING TO PRACTICE ON THE GAME AT HOME, AND–
HI, JUSTIN.
EWIS AND C
–WORK OUT THE LEVELS SO I'M PREPARED FOR–
HEY, JUSTIN!
-- ANYTHING THAT MIGHT COME UP. NO MATTER WHAT THE BOOK SAYS, IT'S–
HEY THERE, JUSTIN!
–NOTHING LIKE PLAYING IT FOR **REAL**. THERE ARE THINGS YOU CAN'T LEARN JUST BY–
WHAT'S UP, JUSTIN?
GAH! ALL RIGHT!
I GOT IT!! EVERYONE LIKES YOU AND NO ONE KNOWS I EXIST!!
JEREMY, I...
LET'S JUST GO HOME.

LATER THAT NIGHT...
C'MON, C'MON...ALMOST THERE...
ZAP FRIZZ
GAME OVER. YOU LOSE.
BOOP!
ARRGH!!
JEREMY...
ARE YOU STILL AWAKE PLAYING THAT VIDEO GAME?
IT'S ONE IN THE MORNING.
UGH. AND IT'S SO HOT IN HERE.
I'M TRYING TO BEAT THE THIRD LEVEL.
I GET RIGHT TO THE END AND THEN I DIE.
LIKE I SAID, I'VE BEEN READING THE BOOK AND–

WHO CARES?!
I DON'T NEED YOUR BOOK OR YOUR HELP!
BUT I'VE BEEN THINKING THAT IF WE BOTH WORK TOGETHER, WE COULD BEAT THE–
DON'T YOU GET IT?!
I DON'T WANT TO DO ANYTHING TOGETHER!
WHAT?
I DON'T WANT YOUR HELP! I DON'T WANT YOU AROUND! I DON'T WANT TO BE A TWIN!
YOU... YOU DON'T MEAN THAT, DO YOU?

JEREMY...?
Y'KNOW, WHEN I WAS BORN, THERE WAS ONE BRIGHT SHINING MOMENT WHERE IT WAS JUST ME.
IT WAS THE BEST ONE SECOND OF MY LIFE!
AND THEN *YOU* CAME ALONG AND *RUINED* IT ALL.
I *HATE* THAT YOU LOOK LIKE ME! I *HATE* THAT PEOPLE ALL WANT TO BE *YOUR* FRIEND! I *HATE* THAT PEOPLE CALL US *"THE TWINS"* OR *"TWINKIES."*
I *HATE* PEOPLE ASKING "WHICH ONE ARE YOU?" BUT MOSTLY I JUST HATE—
GUYS...

ARE YOU STILL PLAYING VIDEO GAMES AT THIS HOUR?!
UM... NOPE!
THWACK!
JUSTIN WAS SLEEP-WALKING AND I WAS... UM... MAKING SURE HE DIDN'T HURT HIMSELF.
WHATEVER...
JUST GO BACK TO BED.
AND I WAS HAVING SUCH A GOOD DREAM.
NEVER GONNA SEE A CHOCOLATE MERRY-GO-ROUND AGAIN.

I'M GOING TO SLEEP.
BUT DO YOU ACTUALLY UNDERSTAND THE THIRD LEVEL?
LOOK, I KNOW WHAT'S NEXT! I'M TIRED! I'M GOING TO—
STOP IT!
STOP WHAT?
SHAKING MY BED!
BUT I'M NOT—
WHOA!
GLORP!
WHAT IS THAT?!
THE NEXT LEVEL, I GUESS!
GAH!
JEREMY!

JEREMY! JEREMY! WHAT CAN I DO?!
STOP LOOKING LIKE ME!!
SPLOOSH
NEXT TIME KEEP THE WINDOW **CLOSED,** GENIUS!
HOW WAS I SUPPOSED TO KNOW-
-THAT A GIANT JELL-O CREATURE WOULD ATTACK IN THE MIDDLE OF THE NIGHT?
I THOUGHT YOU KNEW **EVERYTHING** ABOUT THE GAME FROM THAT BOOK!
UM... YEAH... BUT...

... THIS ISN'T PART OF THE GAME!
WAIT! WHAT? THIS ISN'T SOME SECRET LEVEL?!
NO!
ULP.

WHAT SHOULD I DO?
IT'S A GIANT JELL-O MONSTER!!
UM...UM... I DON'T KNOW. CUT UP SOME FRUIT AND PUT IT IN A MOLD?
SEE? NO HELP AT ALL!
I DON'T KNOW WHY I-
CHOMP!
JEREMY!
HE ATE YOU!

NO KIDDING, CAPTAIN OBVIOUS!
JEREMY, HOW ARE YOU GOING TO **BEAT** THIS THING?
HOW HARD CAN IT BE? IT'S JUST JELL-O!
SPLORT!
J
SPLOOM!
E
SPLAM!
L
SKRUM!
L
OH.
UM...
SEE? TOLD YOU IT WOULDN'T BE HARD.

MORE LIKE J-E-L-L-OH-NO!

BLOOSH!
UGH!
WHOA! ALMOST GOT ME!
JEREMY! LOOK OUT!
SPLAT!
HA HA HA HA HA HA!

BLOOSH!
HEY! JUSTIN, WHY DIDN'T YOU WARN ME?!
JUSTIN?
WHERE'D YOU GO?
GREAT. JUST GREAT. ALL HE WANTS TO DO IS HELP, BUT WHEN I NEED IT, HE RUNS OFF.
WHOOP!
WHAM!

WHOA! THAT WAS **CLOSE.** YOU OKAY, JEREMY?
YEAH, I'M— **HEY!**
WHERE'D YOU GO?! I THOUGHT YOU WERE GONNA HELP!
I AM. I JUST WANTED TO WASH OFF THAT JELL-O.
WASH OFF THE–?
YOU JUST WASHED THE JELL-O AWAY?!
SURE.
JELL-O'S MOSTLY WATER... JUST SPRAY MORE WATER AND IT MELTS AWAY.
DUH. OF COURSE. WHY DIDN'T **I** THINK OF THAT?
WHAT ARE YOU DOING?

GONNA WASH AWAY SOME JELL-O.
SKWEE SKWEE SKWEE
FRTSSHHH
FRTSSHHH
FRTSSHHH
ARRGH!
FRSHH
SSSS
AHH!
ARRGH!
FRTSHH
AHH!

AAAAAAAAAHHH
THAKKATHAKKATHAKKATHAKKATHAKKATHAKKATHAKKATH
AAAAAAAAAAHHH!
THAKKATHAKKATHAKKATHAKKATHAKKATHAKKATHAKKATH
THAKKATHAKKATHAKKATHAKKATHAKKATHAKKATHAKKATH

YES!
OUT OF THE WAY! COSMIC COMMANDO COMING THROUGH!
WHOA!
WOW! THAT WAS AMAZING!
I TOLD YOU I DON'T NEED A BOOK TO SHOW ME WHAT TO DO.
SO, WHAT ARE YOU GOING TO DO NOW?
NOW I GO TO SLEEP.
HOW WEIRD THAT THE JELL-O CREATURE ISN'T IN THE REGULAR GAME.
CLICK
AND WHY DOES IT FEEL LIKE WE FORGOT SOMETHING?
THAKKATHAKKATHAKKATHAKK

CUTSCENE

SKORN!

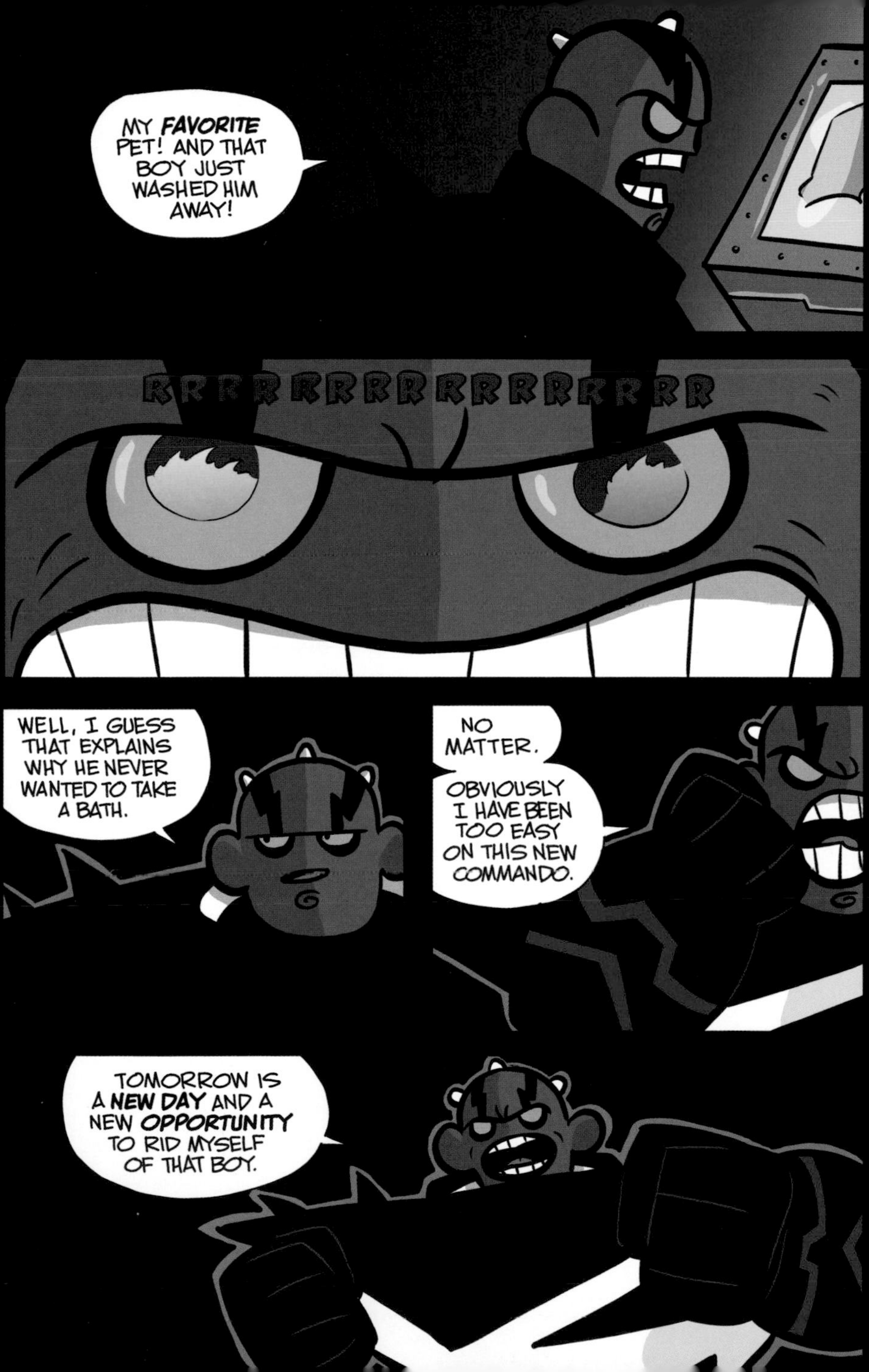
MY **FAVORITE** PET! AND THAT BOY JUST WASHED HIM AWAY!
RRRRRRRRRRRRRRRRR
WELL, I GUESS THAT EXPLAINS WHY HE NEVER WANTED TO TAKE A BATH.
NO MATTER.
OBVIOUSLY I HAVE BEEN TOO EASY ON THIS NEW COMMANDO.
TOMORROW IS A **NEW DAY** AND A NEW **OPPORTUNITY** TO RID MYSELF OF THAT BOY.

THE NEXT MORNING...
AH... NOTHING LIKE A BEAUTIFUL DAY, A CUP OF COFFEE, AND THE MORNING FUNNIES.
#2 *DAD* *WE TRY HARDER
HA HA!
OH, GARFIELD... I HATE MONDAYS, TOO.
SPLASH!
THAKKATHAKK
DRIP
DRIP
DRIP
WHO LEFT THE SPRINKLERS ON?!!

JEREMY! DID YOU LEAVE THE SPRINKLERS ON LAST NIGHT?
ME?
WHY WOULD I-
BECAUSE YOU ALWAYS LEAVE THINGS FOR EVERYONE ELSE TO CLEAN UP!
IT WASN'T JEREMY, DAD. HE WAS IN BED ALL NIGHT.
HMM...
WELL, I KNOW SOMETHING IS UP WITH YOU GUYS. I'VE GOT MY EYE ON YOU.
I KNOW YOU THINK THAT BY HELPING ME, YOU'LL GET TO BE A COSMIC COMMANDO TOO. BUT IT'S NOT GOING TO HAPPEN.
I CAN BEAT THIS GAME ALL BY MYSELF. I DON'T NEED YOUR HELP.
JUST WATCH.

I CAN TOTALLY PLAY THIS GAME ALL BY MYSELF!
I DON'T NEED JUSTIN.
ALL I HAVE TO DO IS PRACTICE ON MY VIDEO GAME TO PREPARE FOR THE REAL THING.
I CAN TOTALLY DO THIS.
RIGHT.
I CAN DO THIS.

AND I STARTED DOING IT **THAT MORNING.**
THE NEXT LEVEL HAD GIANT **ROBOT BUGS.**
THEY WEREN'T **THAT** HARD TO BEAT.
ALL I HAD TO DO WAS **ENLARGE** A CAN OF BUG SPRAY.
AND THE WHOLE TIME I WAS BATTLING IN REAL LIFE, I WAS ALSO PRACTICING BETWEEN LEVELS AT HOME.
FSHHHHHHA
COSMI
ROBOT
BUG
SPRAY

BUT JUST LIKE IN THE GAME, THE REAL-LIFE BATTLES GOT HARDER AND HARDER.
THE ROBO-SQUID WAS TRICKY.
LET'S MAKE SOME CALAMARI.
ALL I NEED TO DO IS DEEP-FRY HIM AND—
SPLURG!
BLOOP BLOOP
WHAT THE—?!
IF MY BLASTERS DON'T WORK UNDERWATER, WHAT AM I GONNA—
BOOM!

GUESS I'M GONNA BE IN A LOT OF PAIN.
OUCH.
MAY AS WELL PUT THIS JET-PACK TO SOME USE.
CHOOM!
SPHLOOM!
HA! THAT SEEMED TO RATTLE HIM...
UM...
HE'S REALLY RATTLING.
WHAT'S HE DOING?

SPLORT!
OH, GREAT.
ROBOTIC SQUID INK.
OR IS IT OIL?
SKROOM!
UGH!
ENERGY
OUCH!
HE CAN STILL HIT ME EVEN THOUGH IT'S PITCH-BLACK.
HOW AM I SUPPOSED TO FIGHT B–
FLOOM!
OOF!

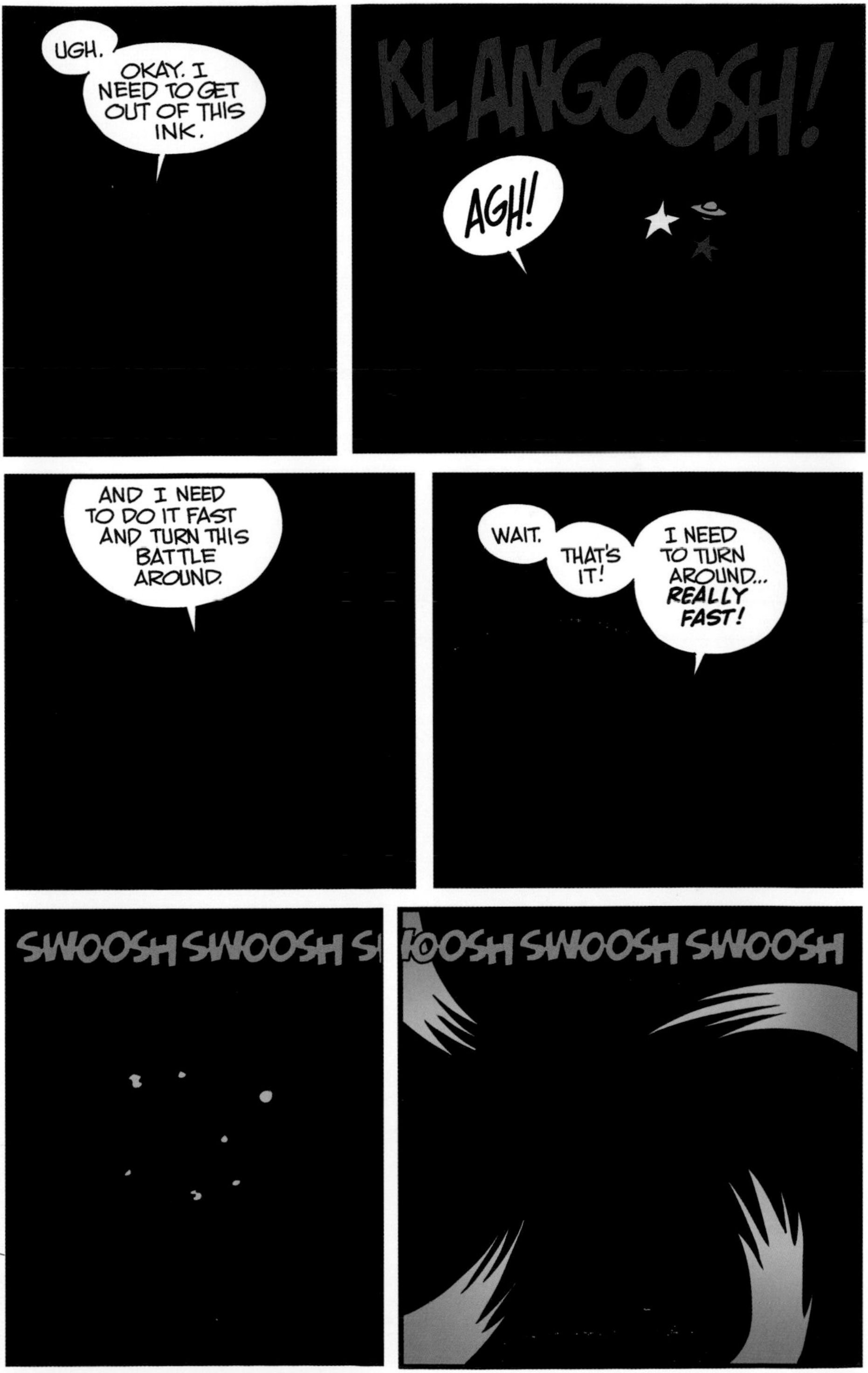
UGH.
OKAY. I NEED TO GET OUT OF THIS INK.
KLANGOOSH!
AGH!
AND I NEED TO DO IT FAST AND TURN THIS BATTLE AROUND.
WAIT.
THAT'S IT!
I NEED TO TURN AROUND... REALLY FAST!
SWOOSH SWOOSH SWOOSH SWOOSH SWOOSH

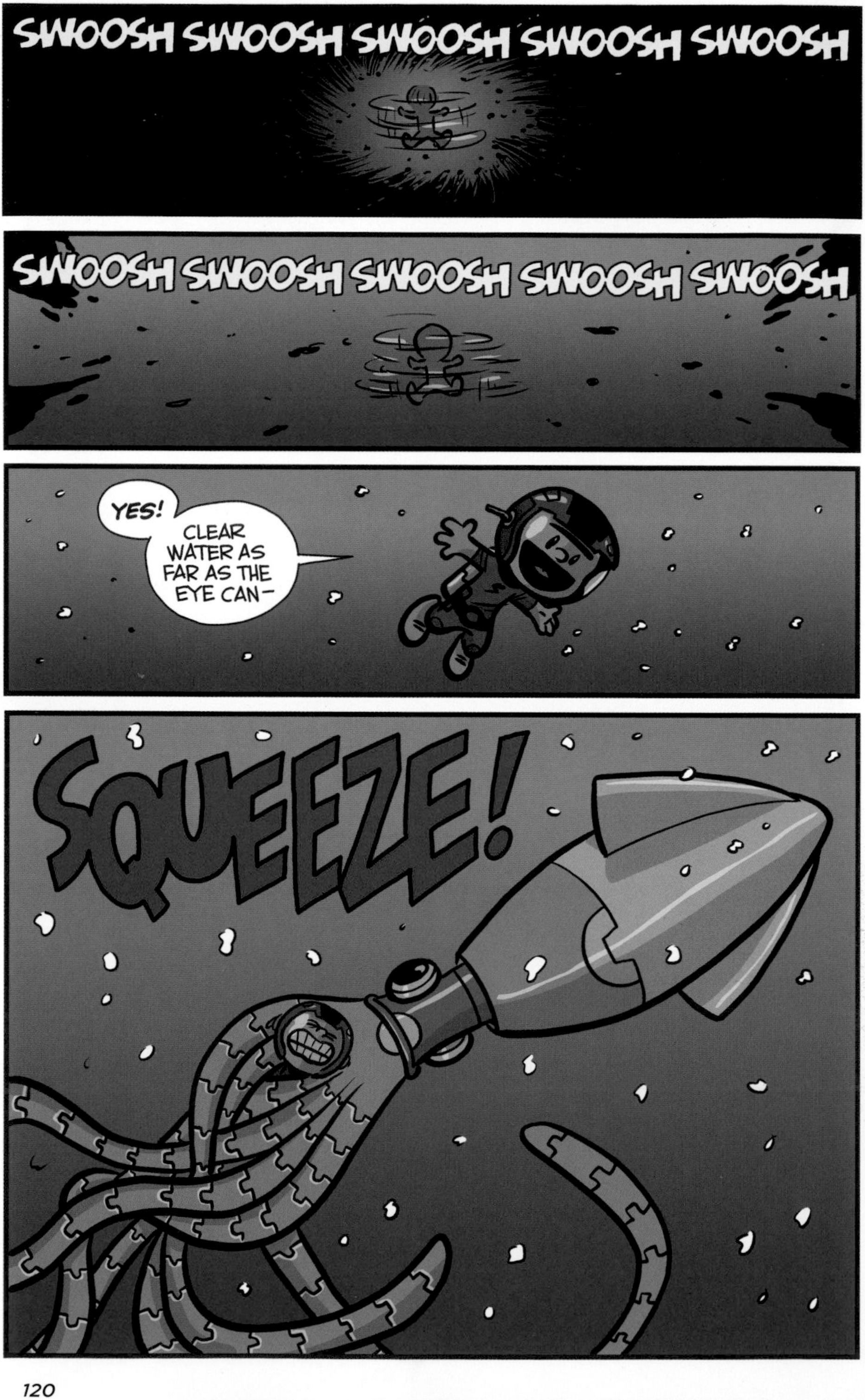
SWOOSH SWOOSH SWOOSH SWOOSH SWOOSH
SWOOSH SWOOSH SWOOSH SWOOSH SWOOSH
YES!
CLEAR WATER AS FAR AS THE EYE CAN–
SQUEEZE!

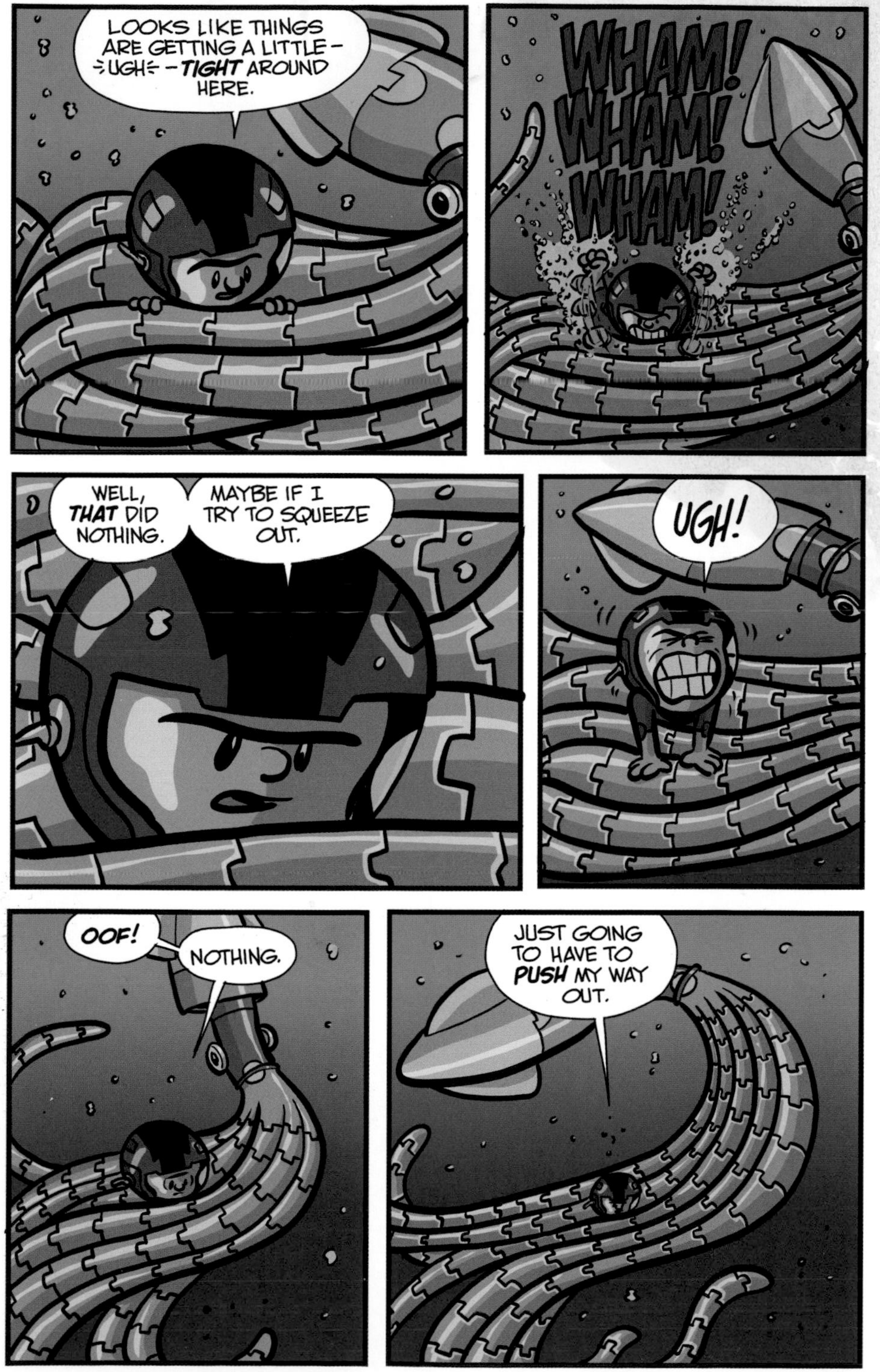

LOOKS LIKE THINGS ARE GETTING A LITTLE— UGH— —TIGHT AROUND HERE.
WHAM! WHAM! WHAM!
WELL, THAT DID NOTHING.
MAYBE IF I TRY TO SQUEEZE OUT.
UGH!
OOF!
NOTHING.
JUST GOING TO HAVE TO PUSH MY WAY OUT.

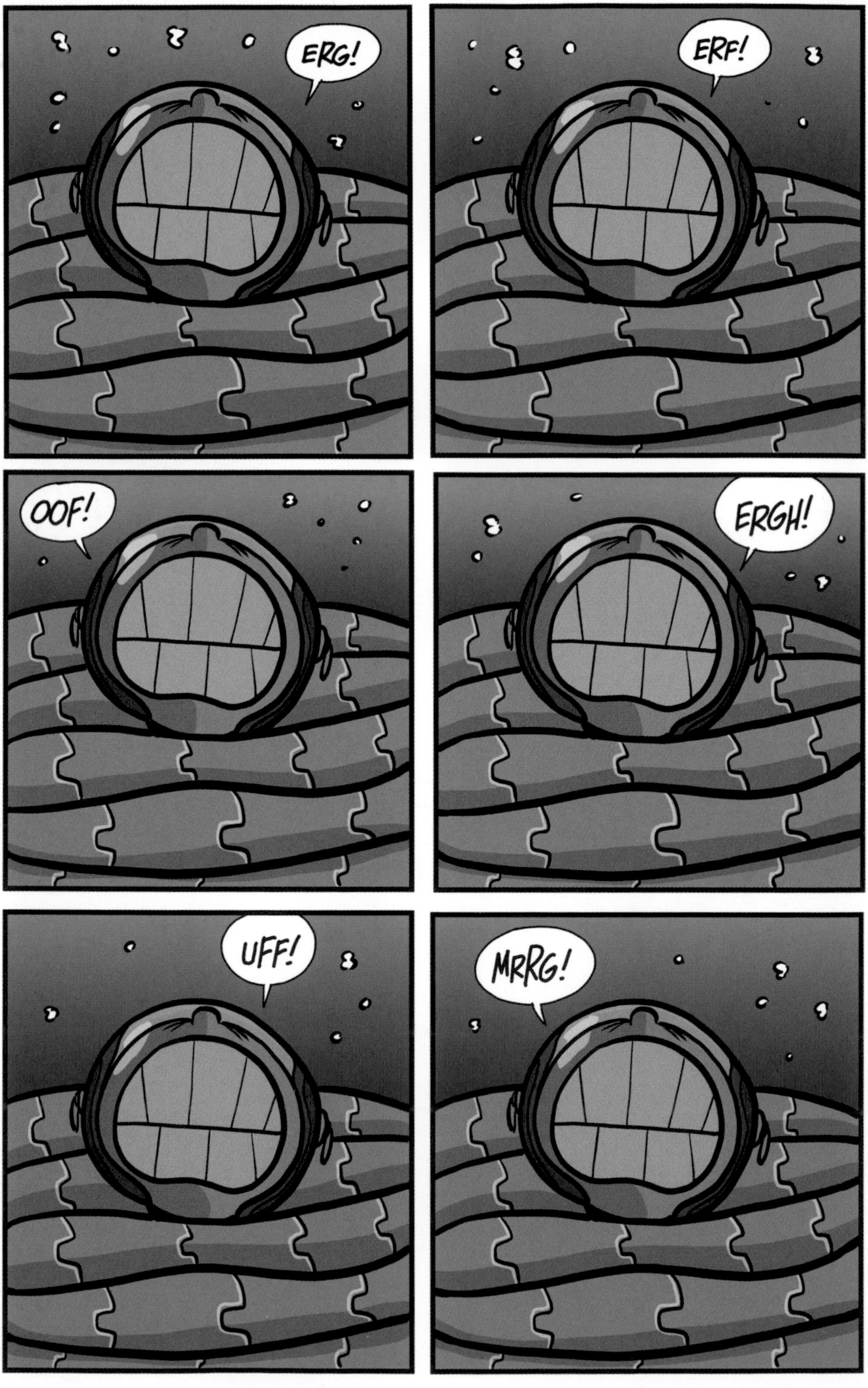
ERG!
ERF!
OOF!
ERGH!
UFF!
MRRG!

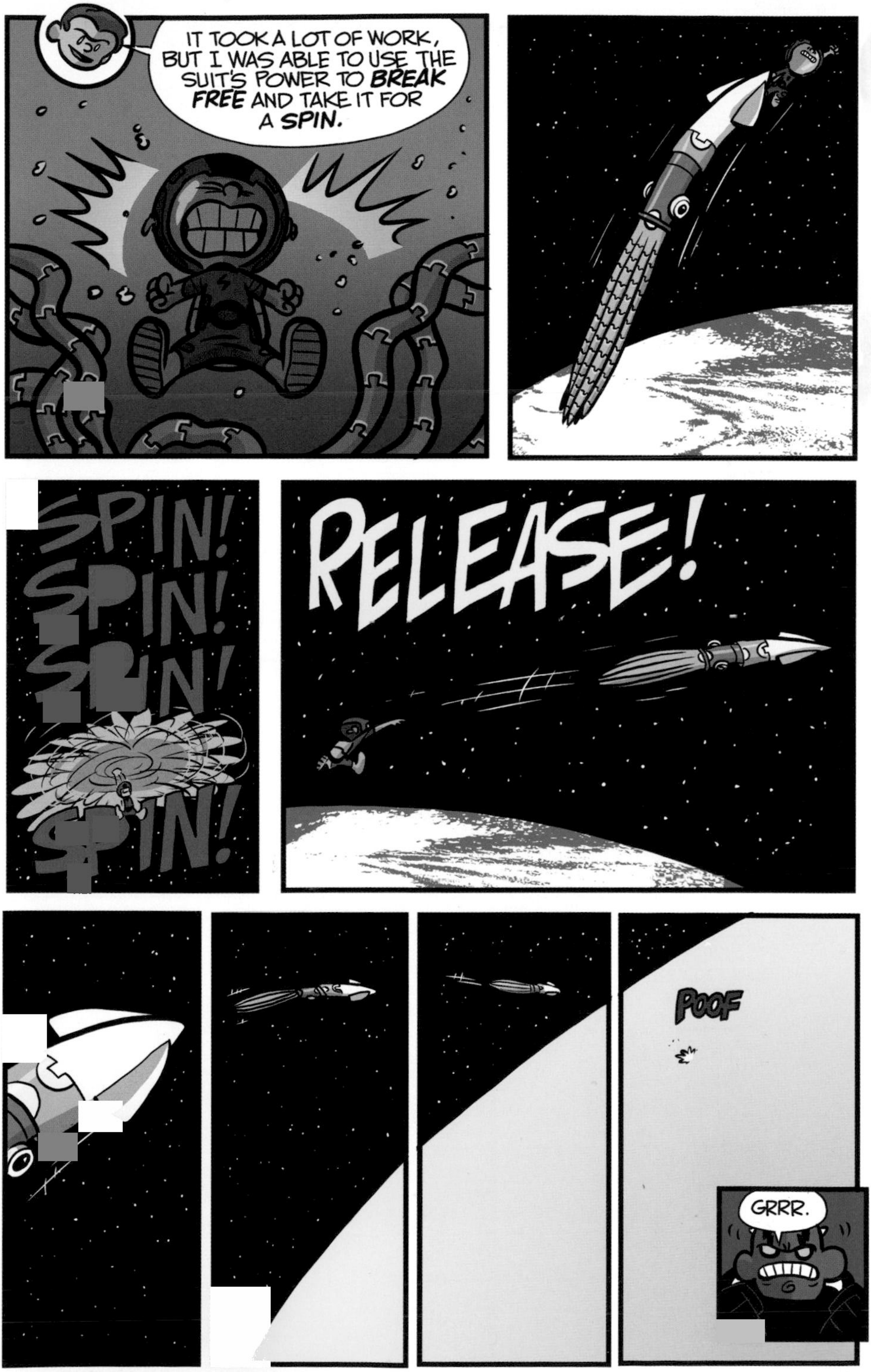
IT TOOK A LOT OF WORK, BUT I WAS ABLE TO USE THE SUIT'S POWER TO **BREAK FREE** AND TAKE IT FOR A **SPIN.**
SPIN!
SPIN!
SPIN!
SPIN!
RELEASE!
POOF
GRRR.

ONE OF THE CRAZIEST LEVELS WAS THE COSMIC GUITAR BATTLE LEVEL.
JUSTIN TRIED TO SHOW ME HOW TO BEAT THE LEVEL, BUT I, OF COURSE TOLD HIM TO...
BEAT IT!!
I ROCKED!!
YOU ROCK!
THERE WAS ONLY ONE PROBLEM...
THE LAST LEVEL.
FINAL MISSION FAILED.
ARRGH!
GAME OVER

WHAT WAS JUSTIN DOING THIS WHOLE TIME?
WHAT DO I CARE?
BECAUSE...
SNIFF

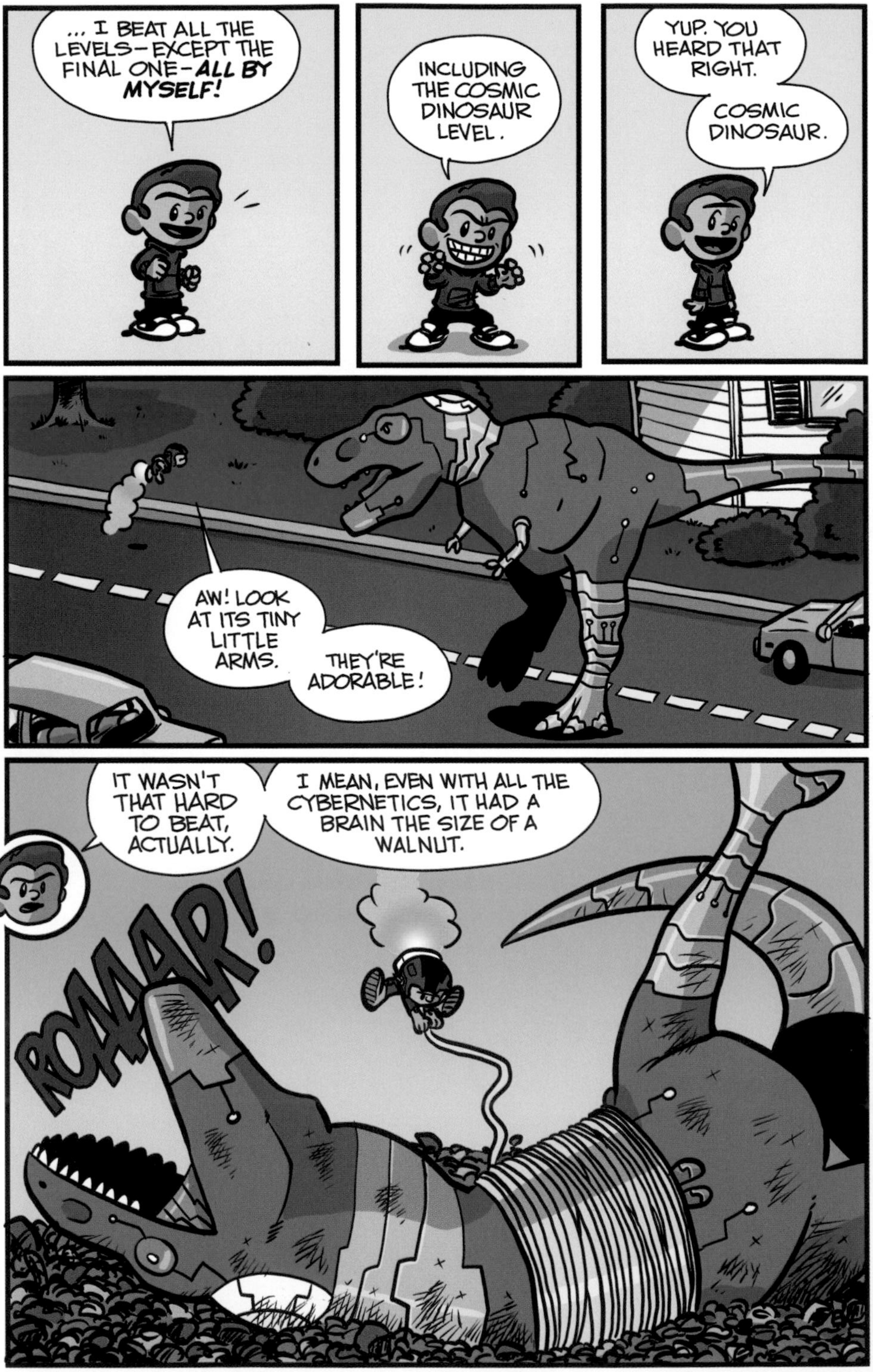
... I BEAT ALL THE LEVELS—EXCEPT THE FINAL ONE—**ALL BY MYSELF!**
INCLUDING THE COSMIC DINOSAUR LEVEL.
YUP. YOU HEARD THAT RIGHT.
COSMIC DINOSAUR.
AW! LOOK AT ITS TINY LITTLE ARMS.
THEY'RE ADORABLE!
IT WASN'T THAT HARD TO BEAT, ACTUALLY.
I MEAN, EVEN WITH ALL THE CYBERNETICS, IT HAD A BRAIN THE SIZE OF A WALNUT.
ROAAAR!

THE DINOSAUR WAS EASY.
THE **FINAL** LEVEL, NOT SO MUCH.
I TRIED **EVERYTHING,** BUT NOTHING WORKED.
AND NOW THE REAL-LIFE GAME HAS CAUGHT UP WITH THE VIDEO GAME.
THE FINAL LEVEL COULD BEGIN AT ANY MOMENT.
I MIGHT HAVE TO DO THE UNTHINKABLE.
I MIGHT HAVE TO ASK FOR **JUSTIN'S** HELP.

CUTSCENE

SKORN!

HOW IS IT POSSIBLE THAT THIS CHILD HAS EASILY DISPATCHED MY MOST LETHAL CREATURES?
THIS HAS GONE ON FAR TOO LONG.
IT IS TIME TO UNLEASH ARMAGEDDON!
TIME TO RELEASE MY ARMADA!
TIME TO END THIS GAME!

CHAPTER SIX

ENDGAME

JEREMY?!
YOU WANT TO SIT WITH... ME?
I THOUGHT YOU DIDN'T WANT ANYONE TO KNOW YOU HAVE A BROTHER.
OKAY, LET'S NOT MAKE A BIG PRODUCTION OUT OF THIS.
CAN I SIT HERE OR NOT?
OF COURSE.
EVERYTHING OKAY?
YEAH, YEAH. FINE.
GAH!

LET ME GUESS. PROBLEM WITH THE FINAL LEVEL?
YES! HOW'D YOU KNOW THAT?
OH, YEAH. THE **GUIDE BOOK.**
WELL, I CAN'T FIGURE IT OUT, AND NOW I'M AT THAT LEVEL IN THE **REAL** GAME.
IT COULD START AT **ANY MINUTE.**
DO **YOU** KNOW WHAT TO DO?
I DO.
BUT YOU'RE **NOT** GOING TO LIKE IT.
I DON'T CARE.
JUST TELL ME SO I CAN–

CHOOM!
WHAT THE–?
KRKKKKK
JEREMY, THE CEILING IS GONNA CAVE IN! YOU NEED TO HOLD IT UP UNTIL EVERYONE GETS OUT!
ON IT!
NOW, GO HOME!
BUT WHAT ABOUT–?
JUST GO!
KRKKKKKKK

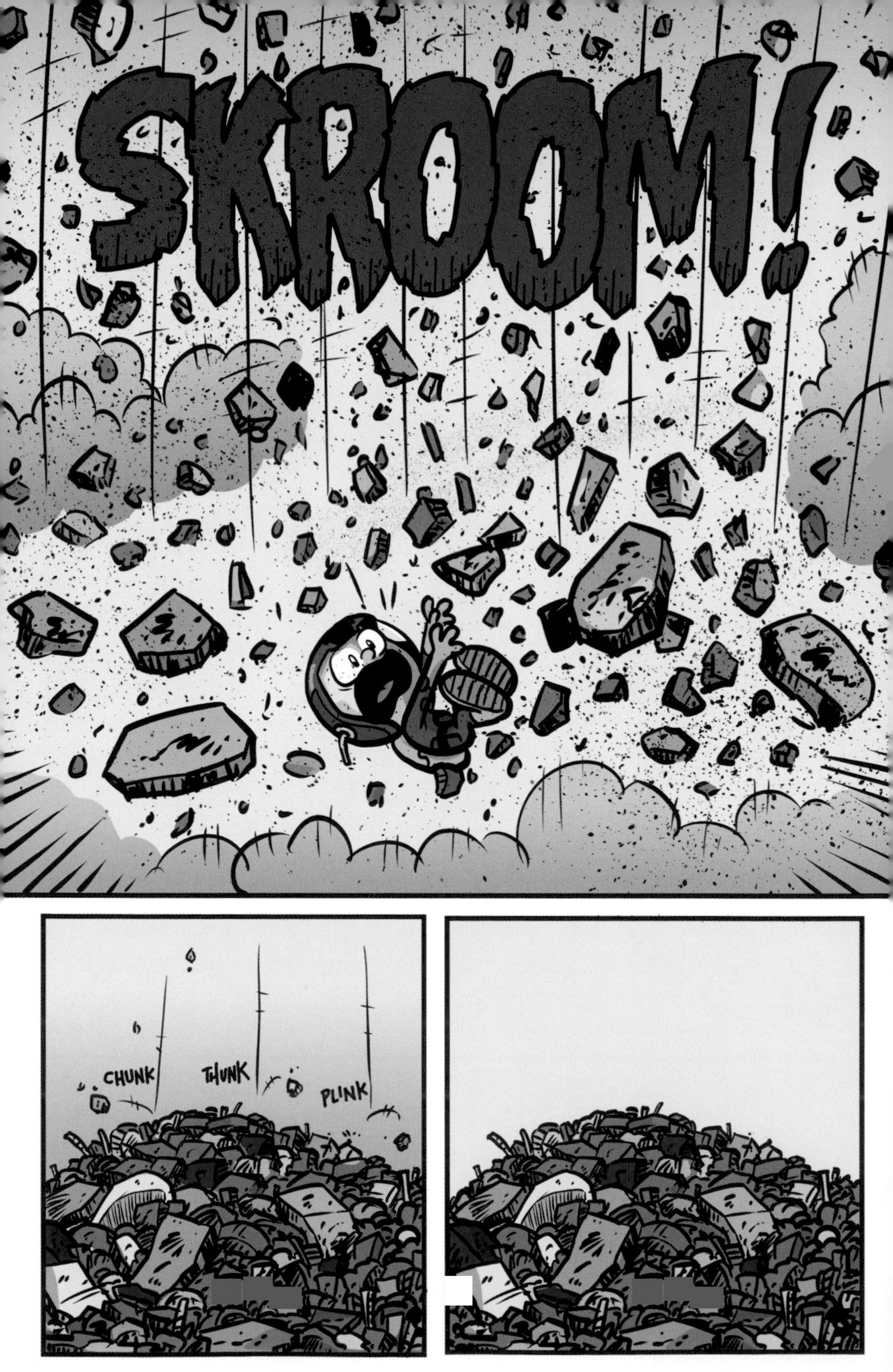
SKROOM!
CHUNK
THUNK
PLINK

BRAKKABABOOM!
JEREMY!! YOU'RE OKAY!!
WHAT ARE YOU STILL DOING HERE?! I TOLD YOU TO GO HOME!
BUT I KNOW HOW TO...
...BEAT THE LAST LEVEL.

WHEW
OKAY, HERE WE GO.
JUST HAVE TO MAKE SURE ALL THE STUDENTS ARE SAFE. (OR MOM WILL KILL ME.)
CAN'T SEE **JUSTIN.** HOPE HE'S OKAY.

1
COSMIC COMMANDO TIPS & TRICKS TO BEAT EVERY LEVEL!

BOOM!

OH NO.
1
COSMIC COMMANDO TIPS & TRICKS TO BEAT EVERY LEVEL!
JEREMY...

MAN, THIS IS **NOT** GOING WELL.
ENERGY
YOW!
ZARK!
THWAKK!
FWAPP!
THUMP!
SKRRRRR
OW!
THOSE BLASTS **REALLY** HURT!
AND THERE ARE SO MANY SHIPS.
BUT I'VE GOTTA BEAT THEM!
JEREMY!

GAH!
TARGET ACQUIRED.
SCANNING.
GENETIC IMPRINT DOWNLOADED.
SUBJECT: COSMIC COMMANDO.
COMMENCE NEURO-WEB DISPERSAL.
JEREMY! I HAVE THE BOOK! I CAN HELP!
GET OFF!
COSMIC COMMANDOS TIPS & TRICKS TO BEAT EVERY LEVEL!
OH, MAN. THIS IS THE PART WHERE I ALWAYS LOSE.
THIS IS GONNA HURT.

FRZAKK!
OOF!
FWAM!
JEREMY, WAIT! I CAN—
NOT NOW!
GET OUT OF HERE!
FRZAKK!
JEREMY!
OOF!
TOOM!
JUST LISTEN TO ME FOR A MINUTE!
UNH... NO, I CAN'T... HAVE... TO...

JEREMY, YOU LISTEN TO ME!
I KNOW THE REASON WHY YOU HAVEN'T BEEN ABLE TO BEAT THE LAST LEVEL!
FINE! WHAT IS IT?
IT'S REALLY A SIMPLE SOLUTION IF YOU JUST THINK ABOUT IT.
ALL YOU HAVE TO DO IS-
LOOK OUT!
SHOVE!

ARGH!
FRZAKAZLAK
JUSTIN!
SHKKKKKKKKK
OH NO!
JUSTIN!
JUSTIN! ***JUSTIN!*** ARE YOU OKAY? SAY SOMETHING!
I... I TOLD YOU TO GET OUT OF HERE.
PLEASE BE OKAY.
SAY SOMETHING...
SCANNING: TWO IDENTICAL GENETIC MARKERS.
CONFUSION.

PLEASE, JUSTIN.
WHAT AM I GOING TO DO WITHOUT YOU?
I'M... I'M SO SORRY FOR THE WAY I'VE TREATED YOU.
I... I DIDN'T MEAN IT.
EVERYONE LIKES YOU AND I WAS JEALOUS AND STUPID. I JUST WANTED TO DO SOMETHING BY MYSELF, THAT NO ONE ELSE COULD DO. THAT'S WHY I WAS SO MEAN TO YOU. I'M SO SORRY, JUSTIN.
AND... AND NOW I'M ALL ALONE AGAINST THESE ALIENS.
I'M SO SCARED, JUSTIN.
I DON'T KNOW WHAT TO DO.
SNIFF
HUHUUH
SOB

JUSTIN!! YOU'RE ALIVE!
...
WHAT DID YOU SAY?
M... MULTIPLAYER...
RIGHT!
GIVE IT A TWIST.

KRAKKABADOOM!

FSSSSSSSSSSSSS

OKAY, JEREMY.
LET'S MASH SOME POTATOES!
DO WHAT?
UM... YOU KNOW... MASH SOME FLYING SAUCER POTATOES.
FLYING SAUCER POTATOES.
THAT'S ONE WEIRD BATTLE CRY.

TIME TO END THIS GAME.
ERROR...ERROR. IDENTICAL GENE MARKER.
STATUS: CONFUSION.
LET'S GO!
FRZAKK!
CHOOM!
CONFUSION...UNABLE TO LOCK ON ONE TARGET.
CONFUSION... CONFUSION... CONFU-

CHOOM!
YEEE-HA!
SAY GOODBYE, RUST-BUCKETS!
JEREMY!
BEHIND YOU!
WHOA!
BRAKOOM!
YOU WERE RIGHT, JUSTIN — THIS IS MUCH BETTER WITH A PARTNER.
BUT THERE'S NO TIME TO CELEBRATE! WE'VE GOT WORK TO DO!

ZRAKK!
CHOOM!
ZRAPP!
SCORE!!
BRADOOM!

BOOM!
CHOOM!
BA-DOOM!
CHOOM! CHOOM!
SKROOM!
THROOM!

BRAKKA-BA-DOOM!

YES!
WE DID IT!
YEAH!
YEAH!
AWESOME!
AMAZING!
UM... IS SOMETHING SUPPOSED TO HAPPEN?
YES...

...NOW I WILL DESTROY YOU!
WHO IS THAT, JEREMY?
SKORN. THE BAD GUY.
I DON'T REMEMBER HIM HAVING EARS THAT BIG.
BUT HE NEVER APPEARS IN THE GAME.
THIS IS NO GAME, FOOLS.
AND MY EARS AREN'T THAT BIG.
WHATEVER MAGIC YOU USED AFFORDED ME THE OPPORTUNITY TO ESCAPE THE CONFINES OF THAT DIGITAL PRISON.
AS LONG AS YOU DON'T WIN, I AM FREE TO CONQUER THIS WORLD!
YOU MAY HAVE BEATEN MY MINIONS, BUT YOU WILL SOON LEARN THE TASTE OF DEFEAT!

GAH!
LOOK OUT!
BECAUSE YOU NOW MUST FACE ME!
BRAKKABATHOOM!

A FACE WITH GIANT EARS.
JUSTIN! DOES THE BOOK MENTION ANY OF THIS?

NO...BUT IF I'M RIGHT, UNLESS WE BEAT SKORN...

CHOOM!
THE WHOLE TOWN IS TOAST!!
JEREMY, I'LL GET HIGH. YOU GET LOW AND START BLASTING!
NO, JUSTIN! THAT'LL ONLY—
SKROOM!!
FZAKK!
ZRAKK!

HAHAHAHAHAHA!
!
...MAKE HIM BIGGER!
ALONG WITH THOSE EARS.

WHAT DO WE DO? IF WE CAN'T **BLAST** HIM, WHAT'S LEFT?
SEE, JUSTIN. THAT'S THE DIFFERENCE BETWEEN **READING** HOW TO DO SOMETHING AND **ACTUALLY** DOING IT.
THERE ARE OTHER THINGS WE CAN USE.
LIKE WHAT?
SHHH. THE **FREEZE RAY.** DUH.
I CAN HEAR YOU.
GULP
THOSE EARS!
A-B-UP-UP-UP!
FREEZE!

SEE? SIMPLE.
TOO COOL FOR SCHOOL!
!
!
KKK
UH-OH.
KKRRRK
KRKKK
SKROOM!

FOOLISH CHILD. YOU THINK FROZEN WATER IS A MATCH FOR SKORN, DEVOURER OF CITIES?!
IMAGINE THE SIZE OF HIS EAR WAX.
LIKE ROACHES, YOU COMMANDOS MAY MULTIPLY, BUT I CAN EASILY DEFEAT YOU BOTH.
CHOOM!
GAH!
WHOA!
I HAVE CONQUERED WORLDS!
ZRAKK!
DESTROYED PLANETS!
BOOOM!
WHAT ARE TWO LITTLE CHILDREN TO THE LIKES OF ME?!

NOTHING!
THE SCHOOL!
MOM'S GONNA KILL US!
KROOM!
JEREMY, WHAT ARE WE GOING TO DO?!
WE'RE GONNA HAVE TO TRY ALL THE OTHER SPECIAL MOVES!
LIKE WHAT?!

HEAT RAY!
LASERS!
GRAVITY PULSE!

ELECTROMAGNETIC PULSE!
VIBRO-SOUND BLAST!
HAHAHA!
NOTHING YOU DO CAN HARM ME!
IT ONLY MAKES ME STRONGER!
AND HIS EARS HUGER!

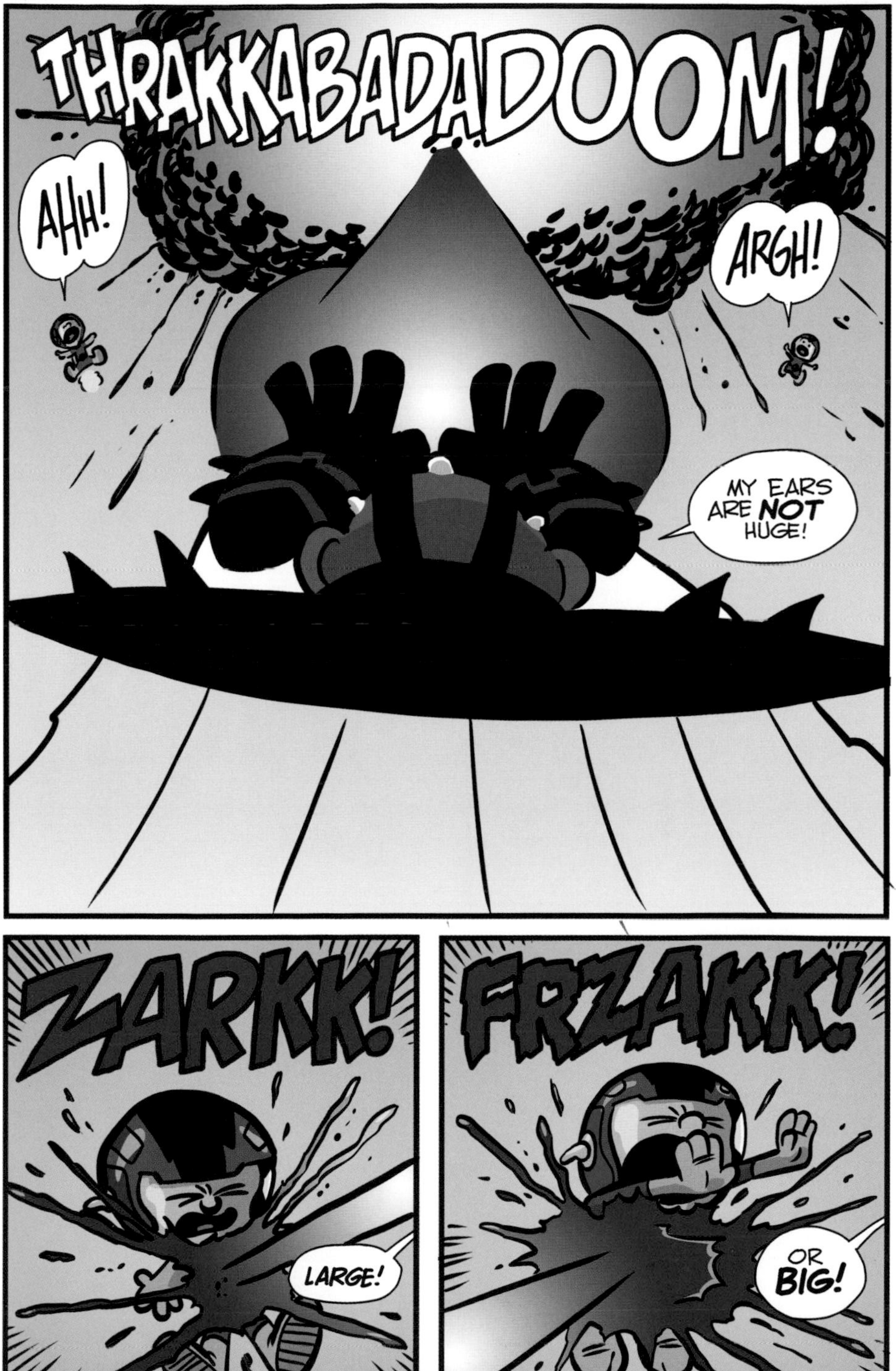
THRAKKABADADOOOM!
AHH!
ARGH!
MY EARS ARE **NOT** HUGE!
ZARKK!
LARGE!
FRZAKK!
OR BIG!

OH, MAN, JEREMY. LOOK AT OUR ENERGY LEVELS!
ENERGY
ENERGY
AND IF THEY GO DOWN TO NOTHING—
THEN IT'S GAME OVER FOR US!
WELL, LET'S GET HIM BEFORE THAT HAPPENS!
FRZARKK!
SKROOM!
C'MON!
ENERGY
ENERGY

SKROOM!
ENERGY
UHF.
OOF.
ENERGY
ENERGY
ENERGY
FRZAKK!
ENERGY
ENERGY
ZRAKK!
JUSTIN, WHAT ARE WE GOING TO DO?
TIME IS GETTING SHORT!
ENERGY
ENERGY
SHORT!
THAT'S IT!!
WHAT'S "IT"?
ENERGY
ENERGY

C'MON! FOLLOW ME!
BACK FOR MORE, MY LITTLE FRIENDS?
YOU KNOW YOU CAN'T POSSIBLY DEFEAT ME!
DO YOU HAVE ANY FINAL WORDS BEFORE I CRUSH YOU INTO DUST?
I DO.
JUST TWO.
CODY SMALLS.
WHAT?
YES!

UP-
DOWN-
A-A-B-
DOWN!
NOW!
UGH!

WHAT-
UNG-
WHAT IS
THIS?

IT'S
WORKING!!
HE'S SHRINKING,
JUSTIN!!

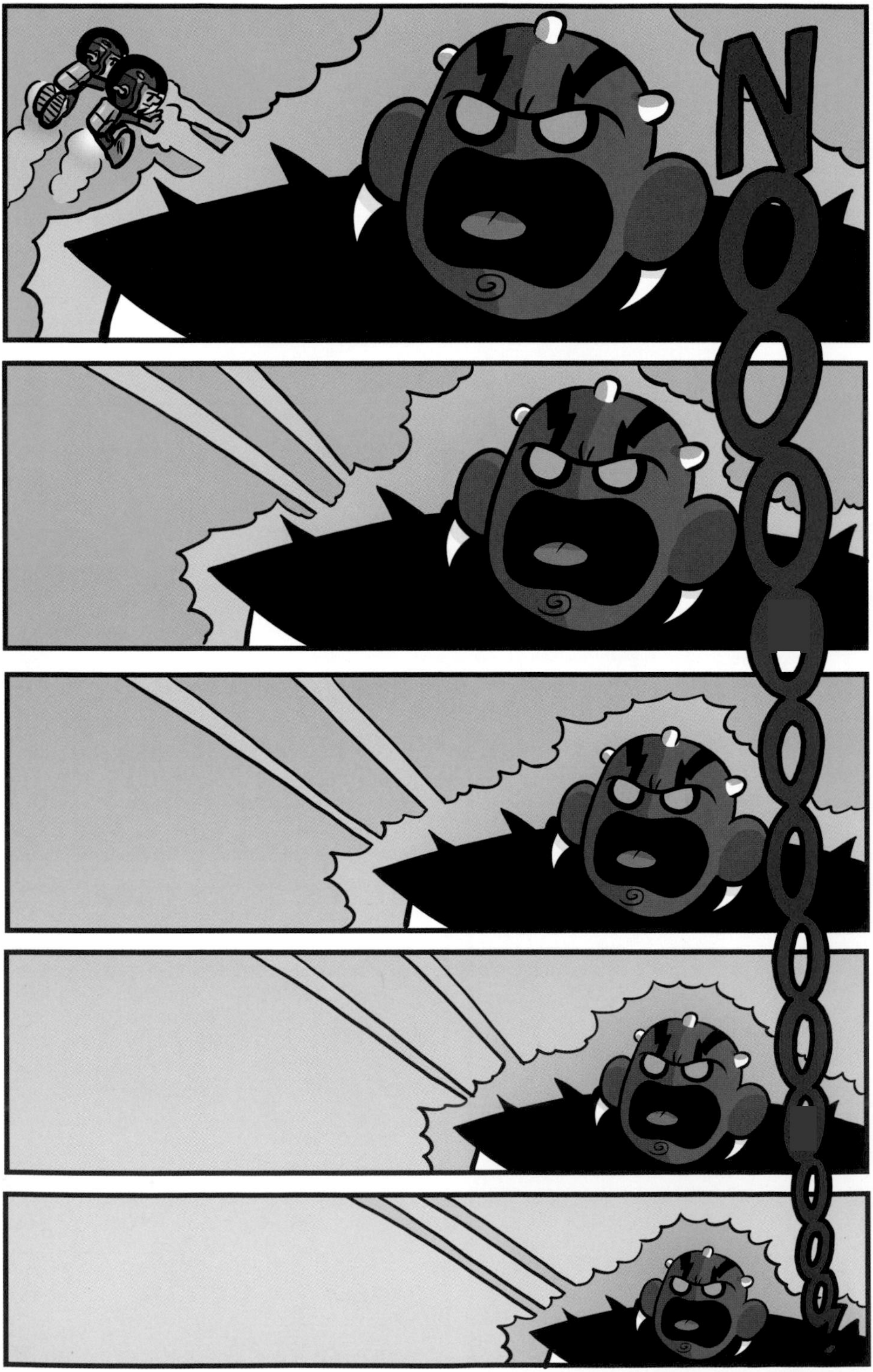
NOOOOOOOOOOOOOOOOO

ENOUGH!
FSHAM!
I DON'T KNOW HOW YOU DID THAT, BUT IT ENDS NOW!
YOU GOT THAT RIGHT, SKORN!
THIS ENDS NOW!

THWOOM!
UGH!
HANG ON! HE'S FIGHTING BACK!
ERG!
SKROOM!
PLEASE, SKORN! JUST STOP THIS!
WE PROMISE, WE'LL LET YOU GO!
YOU JUST LEAVE US AND THE PLANET ALONE AND WE'LL NEVER BOTHER YOU AGAIN.
YOU WOULD DO THAT?
YEAH... YEAH. OF COURSE.
WELL THEN...

DOOM!
...YOU ARE FOOLS!

THIS IS IT, JUSTIN. ABOUT OUT OF ENERGY.
WE NEED TO LAY IT ON...
ENERGY
ENERGY

...TOGETHER!

FRZZZZZZT
IT'S TOO **HARD!** HE'S FIGHTING BACK!
BUT **WE** CAN DO THIS!
C'MON, UP-DOWN-A-A-B-DOWN!

YOU WILL NOT DEFEAT ME THAT EASILY!
UGH!
JEREMY, HE'S STILL FIGHTING BACK. I DON'T KNOW WHAT TO DO!
IT'S OKAY, JUSTIN. I'M GOING TO USE THE FREEZE RAY WHILE YOU KEEP SHRINKING HIM.
CAN'T LEARN THAT IN A BOOK!
NO!

KEEP FIGHTING!
ALMOST THERE!
HE'S GOING MICROSCOPIC!
ALMOST-

BWOOP!

CHAPTER SEVEN

GAME OVER

JEREMY...
JEREMY?
JEREMY?
WHAT... WHAT HAPPENED?
DID WE...?

WE WON!
SKORN POPPED OUT OF EXISTENCE!
IT'S OVER!
THE GAME IS **DONE** AND WE **WON**!
WE WON?!
DOES THAT MEAN—
HEY!
OUR UNIFORMS!
THEY'RE **GONE**!
YUP.
AND ALL THE DAMAGE WAS **REPAIRED**.
IT'S LIKE IT **NEVER** HAPPENED.

AT LEAST I STILL HAVE—
THE RING!
IT'S GONE!
IT FELL OFF!!
COME ON! I'LL HELP YOU FIND IT!
NO, JUSTIN.
NO? BUT IT'S GOT TO BE AROUND HERE SOME—
NO. LET IT GO.
LET IT GO? BUT THE GAME—
WE HAVE THE VIDEO GAME AT HOME.

BESIDES, I THINK I'VE HAD ENOUGH OF COSMIC COMMANDOS.
OKAY.
WELL, I'M GONNA HEAD HOME.
JUSTIN...?
YEAH?
I... I JUST WANTED TO SAY... Y'KNOW, I JUST THOUGHT I'D...
THANK YOU FOR SAVING ME.

I DON'T KNOW **WHAT** I WOULD'VE DONE WITHOUT YOU.
MAYBE I JUST NEED TO BE LIKE **YOU** AND **READ** MORE.
ARE YOU **KIDDING?!** YOU WERE **AMAZING!** YOU CAN DO **ANYTHING!** I COULDN'T BELIEVE HOW YOU WERE ABLE TO DO ALL THAT!!
FIGURING IT OUT AS YOU WENT AND TOTALLY **KICKING BUTT!**
YOU'RE **INCREDIBLE!**
YEAH, WELL, I GUESS WE MAKE A GOOD TEAM, HUH?
THE BEST.
I... I WAS **REALLY** SCARED THERE.
I KNOW.
HUG!

AND STOP LOOKING LIKE ME.
HEH.
Y'KNOW, IT'S NOT SO BAD BEING AN IDENTICAL TWIN.
YEAH?
AT LEAST YOU ALWAYS KNOW WHAT YOUR BEST FRIEND LOOKS LIKE.
SO, I GUESS THIS ISN'T SUCH A **STINKISH** LIFE, HUH?
NOPE...
IT'S REALLY **NOT** STINKISH AT ALL.
SO...

...WHAT DO YOU SAY WE GO HOME AND PLAY **ANOTHER** GAME?
REALLY?
BOTH OF US?
TOGETHER?
TOGETHER.
WE'RE GONNA PLAY A TWO-PLAYER GAME?
YOU **AND** ME?
FOR THE REST OF OUR LIVES, JUSTIN.
FOR THE REST OF OUR LIVES.

EPILOGUE
NEXT PLAYER
HEY! A RING!

JUST NEED TO PUT IT ON...
HMM. A LITTLE TIGHT.
MAYBE IF I GIVE IT A LITTLE TWIST, IT'LL—
FRZZKKK!
REBOOT

MANY THANKS go to so many people who stood by me, guiding and helping me to get this book into your hands. My parents and sister for providing a childhood that bred and nurtured a cartoonist. My friends all along the way who helped shape me: Vincent Pizzuto, Mike Jung, Jimmy Chin, Jody Gross, Anthony Avon, Kenny Lopez, Buddy Scalera, Joe Caramagna, Cory Petit, Clayton Cowles, Joe Sabino, Travis Lanham, Sue Crespi, Dan Carr, Beci Mahnken, Mike Scopa, Michelle Scribner-MacLean, Len Testa, Mike Newell, Erik Larsen, and too many more to name.

Thanks to Robert Snyder for setting up the color files for me. He helped me immensely.

Special thanks to designer Jason Henry, who did an amazing job bringing this book together. He's the secret weapon.

To Lauri Hornik and everyone at Dial Books for bringing me in, taking care of me, and being as excited about this book as I was.

To my inner circle: Nate Cosby, Brad Meltzer, and Judd Winick. They are like brothers to me, and I know they always have my back like I have theirs.

To Jodi Reamer, my agent and my friend. She takes no grief from me and keeps me on the straight and narrow. She leads the way.

To my boys, Jeremy and Justin, the inspiration for this book. They mean more to me than I could ever say, and this book is theirs to always remind them that their father loves them more than the whole wide world.

Finally, to my wife, Audra, who is my sun, my moon, and my stars. She's the only person I ever want to impress and the only person I could ever want to laugh with, cry with, and grow old with. You are my everything.

CHRISTOPHER ELIOPOULOS started his career in comic books, writing and/or drawing books like *Franklin Richards: Son of a Genius*, *Pet Avengers,* and *Cow Boy*. He's currently the illustrator of the *New York Times* bestselling series Ordinary People Change the World, which is written by Brad Meltzer. He lives in New Jersey with his wife and identical twin sons, and hates writing in the third person. You can find him online on twitter @ChrisEliopoulos or at www.chriseliopoulos.com.